*It didn't take a brain surgeon to figure out that
there was some chemistry happening here.*

From the nervous smile on Max's chiseled face
to the way his dark eyes darted up and down,
drinking in Elizabeth from head to toe, he was
clearly quite taken with her. And as for Elizabeth,
well, her flushed cheeks combined with the embarrassed yet at the same time curious look in her
eyes was a dead giveaway. *We have a love connection,* Vanessa thought. *How charming.*

And how utterly unrealistic!

"Who was that?" Elizabeth whispered as Max
traipsed down to the kitchen.

"You haven't figured it out?" Vanessa was incredulous. "It's Max Pennington. Son of the earl.
The future Lord Pennington himself."

"He seems much nicer than I expected,"
Elizabeth remarked as the girls took the final
flight of stairs to the fourth floor.

"That's just an act," Vanessa explained.
"Remember that."

Bantam Books in the Elizabeth series.
Ask your bookseller for the books you have missed.

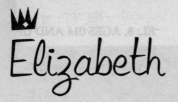

Elizabeth

London Calling

WRITTEN BY
LAURIE JOHN

CREATED BY
FRANCINE PASCAL

BANTAM BOOKS
NEW YORK • TORONTO • LONDON • SYDNEY • AUCKLAND

LONDON CALLING
A Bantam Book / February 2001

Sweet Valley High® *and Sweet Valley University*®
are registered trademarks of Francine Pascal.
Elizabeth is a trademark owned by Francine Pascal.
Conceived by Francine Pascal.

Produced by 17th Street Productions,
an Alloy Online, Inc. company.
33 West 17th Street
New York, NY 10011.

ISBN: 0-553-49354-X

Visit us on the Web! www.randomhouse.com/teens

Published simultaneously in the United States and Canada

Bantam Books is an imprint of Random House Children's Books, a division
of Random House, Inc. BANTAM BOOKS and the rooster colophon are
registered trademarks of Random House, Inc. Bantam Books, 1540
Broadway, New York, New York 10036.

PRINTED IN THE UNITED STATES OF AMERICA

OPM   0 9 8 7 6 5 4 3 2 1

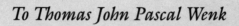

To Thomas John Pascal Wenk

Chapter One

"And this is the right wing of the first floor of Pennington House, where the earl's office is as well as the main ballroom and library," eighteen-year-old Vanessa Shaw droned, her voice stiff with boredom, her almond-shaped brown eyes dulled and flat, jaded. After all, showing people around Pennington House at the end of a hard day's work was hardly Vanessa's idea of entertainment.

Particularly when that person was the new kitchen maid, Elizabeth Bennet, a girl who already in her short acquaintance with Vanessa had proved herself to be a pain in the neck.

"Wow," Elizabeth breathed, panting as she rounded the staircase and entered the ballroom. "What a beautiful wing," she continued reverently, taking in the plush, bloodred carpeting, the oil portraits of the earl of Pennington's lineage lining

1

the walls, the wallpaper threaded through with spun gold, reflecting off the crystal beads of a huge chandelier that hung from the high, vaulted ceiling.

Vanessa flashed Elizabeth a sullen look. The girl was annoying in the extreme, all wide-eyed and impressed and reverent. And then there was the way she looked: so fresh and scrubbed and pearly blond—even though she'd been caught out in the downpour just fifteen minutes ago. Everything about Elizabeth screamed earnestness, and Vanessa was not in the mood for earnestness. And she was especially not up for playing tour guide to some young American with title worship.

"What's the family like?" Elizabeth inquired eagerly, her bright blue-green eyes shining with fascination.

Title worship. Vanessa set her small, plump-lipped mouth in a hard line and quickened her pace as she led Elizabeth out of the ballroom and down the long corridor. *Only an American . . . ,* she thought, irked. Only an American could marvel over the myth of the aristocracy, romanticize the royals, breathe reverently at their bloody wallpaper! The whole thing disgusted Vanessa and made her want to slap the curiosity out of Elizabeth's soft face. And a soft face it was. So American girl next door. So sweet and sensitive.

Like those girls on that cutesy American series that Alice loved to watch on the telly, *Dawson's Creek*. The kind of clear-eyed perfection Vanessa instinctively loathed.

"What are they like?" Vanessa repeated Elizabeth's question, her mouth twisting into a cold smile of contempt. "They're like all the rest is what they're like!" She blazed down the corridor, enjoying the sounds of Elizabeth struggling to catch up. "The earl is a boor and a bore and has a mouth like a chain saw. Watch yourself or he'll bite your head off!"

Good, Vanessa thought, smiling inwardly at Elizabeth's expression. She'd visibly blanched at Vanessa's words. "And as for his children, Sarah and Max, well, they're absolutely monstrous!"

Excellent! Vanessa couldn't help enjoying Elizabeth's expression. She was like a steadily deflating balloon. "If you don't mind your p's and q's around here," Vanessa continued, stamping on the stairs as she made her way up, "you're toast. Believe me, these people are as soulless as they are spoiled. They're a nightmare to work for, and the atmosphere here is one of complete fear. . . ."

As she gabbed on about Pennington House and its inhabitants, Vanessa threw in a few extra tidbits: The earl hated all the staff and wouldn't lower himself to look you in the eye. If you were ever caught using the main staircase instead of the servants' staircase, you'd be fired without pay. If you were caught standing, the earl would fire you because he's paranoid about eavesdropping . . . *blah blah blah.* . . .

Naturally she was exaggerating. Life in Pennington House was no worse than life in the real world. Vanessa knew that all too well, and she dismissed an unwanted memory of being cold and hungry and being forced to wait in a smoky, smelly bar until her mother finished downing her fifteenth drink of the night. "A quick toot," that's what her mother had always called it. . . .

"I'm not sure I can handle this," Elizabeth murmured, breaking into Vanessa's train of thought as they swept past a giant parlor and down a never-ending passage of studies and libraries. "The family sounds dreadful."

"I see you have good listening skills," Vanessa retorted caustically. "That will come in handy. Because every single day here you get lectured at. Either by Cook or by the housekeeper, Mary Dale. It's a Pennington House tradition. Just like the zipped lip."

"Zipped lip?" Elizabeth looked genuinely worried now as they paused outside the billiard room.

"Zipped lip is key to staying employed as a servant," Vanessa explained, trying to suppress a smile. "If you ever open your mouth and try and defend yourself while being accused of something, you're out on your arse, know what I mean? Speak when spoken *to*, not when spoken *at*, get it?"

"I—I . . . guess so," Elizabeth stammered, her eyes darting nervously from side to side.

"Remember, Elizabeth, you're a scullery maid now," Vanessa hissed as they pressed on and up to the second-floor staircase. "Wherever and whoever you were in Smalltown, USA, or whatever it's called that you're from, you're just a girl with a sponge and bucket here. Got that?"

Let up a little, Vanessa's inner voice protested as Elizabeth looked more and more crestfallen with each harsh word from Vanessa's mouth. But it was a feeble protest. After all, it was mostly true in spirit if not in fact. There were certainly enough Pennington rules and regs to easily allow Vanessa to monologue away until her seventy-fifth birthday. And okay, so maybe she was spicing them up a bit, highlighting the highlights rather colorfully, but Vanessa felt strongly about her work: which is to say she detested everything about Pennington House and the family who owned it. And she wasn't about to talk them up to some new servant-to-be. Especially when the girl was herself a pest, not to mention a bit of an odd bod.

Elizabeth Bennet. Please. Vanessa had snorted when she'd first heard the Jane Austen heroine's name and seen Elizabeth's pretty and privileged face. Not to mention those hands. ("Yes, I'm familiar with kitchen work. . . .") Vanessa shook her head. The girl had never touched a mop in her life! *What a crock!* All of which only increased her desire to horrify Elizabeth with tales of life as a scullery maid so grim, they'd horrify a Victorian chimney sweep!

"Vanessa?"

At the touch of Elizabeth's cool hand on her arm, Vanessa stopped her fast-paced walk and reluctantly turned. "What is it? We have a lot more ground to cover, you know," she snapped.

"I think I may be in too deep," Elizabeth replied urgently, her eyes clouded with worry. "Really. I think perhaps you're wasting your time giving me the tour. Sounds like I won't last a minute, let alone a day."

Half amused and half annoyed, Vanessa swatted Elizabeth's arm away. "Relax!" she replied with a dry laugh as they passed the earl's sumptuous suite. "You Americans believe everything you hear. Trust me, you *are* actually allowed to breathe here! Tip: Take what I say with a grain of salt. Not a teaspoon," she added gruffly, "a grain."

Marginally relieved, Elizabeth managed a small

smile on her still fearful face. Which made Vanessa smile, a secret smirk she didn't want Elizabeth to see. This was exactly where Vanessa wanted her. Not too terrified, else she'd quit. *And where's the fun in that?*

No, Vanessa didn't want that. For one, they needed another scullery maid, and Vanessa could sure as heck use the extra hands, soft or no. Also, she wanted Elizabeth to stay because it might be mildly entertaining to watch Miss California or wherever she was from make faux pas in front of the fam-damily! Life here was tedious enough, and Vanessa's eyes glinted at the thought of Elizabeth doing something embarrassing, like curtsying to Lady Sarah. . . .

"You'll be fine," Vanessa said coolly as she guided Elizabeth up to the third floor. But she didn't want Elizabeth to get too comfy. *Where's the fun in that?* No, she would enjoy making Elizabeth do the odd bit of squirming. Like now. "Yes, you'll survive," Vanessa repeated, "but overall, you'll have a none too easy time here. Might as well be honest about that!"

"Well, okay, but if you think I'll make it through." Elizabeth smiled tentatively. "I mean, if you say so, then maybe I will."

Oh, she was just so coy and sweet, it was nauseating! "Didn't say that," Vanessa muttered back.

Scarily, this girl might be trying to befriend her. And Vanessa did not need a friend. Not here, and sure as hell not now! She had important things to do, and she needed to do those things alone. No use having someone around watching her, snooping on her private time, butting into her business . . .

"On your left, the earl's slob-of-a-son Max's bedroom." Vanessa hurriedly returned to her tour-guide program, fearing that Elizabeth might try to bond with her in some way. "As you can see, it's positively palatial. Bitch to clean too, what with all that leather everywhere. Luckily that's not a part of your job or mine. Kitchen only, for us."

"How long have you been working here?" Elizabeth ventured as Vanessa strode purposefully toward the third-floor servants' staircase, eager to get on with it. *Oh, great, personal-chat time.*

"Six months," Vanessa barked brusquely. *A life sentence,* she thought. "But I'll be out of here soon," she added decisively, lifting her chin. *I damned well will!* Though of course much needed to be done before she could get to that point. She had to—

"Pardon, sorry."

Vanessa turned to see that the speaker in question, twenty-one-year-old Maxwell Pennington, had evidently just wheeled around the balustrade of the main stairwell at top speed and practically knocked Elizabeth off her feet.

"I'm awfully sorry," Max repeated, concern and awkwardness vying for dominance in his face. "Are you all right?"

"Yes, I'm fine. It's okay, really," Elizabeth protested with a sweet smile as Max moved to steady her with a hand at her elbow.

"I'm afraid it's my penchant for Häagen-Dazs," Max explained sheepishly. "When I get my after-dinner cravings for cherry chocolate, I just bullet down the stairs, and woe betide anyone who gets in my way! Awfully rude really, sorry."

He laughed a little, nervously. So did Elizabeth.

Vanessa rolled her eyes. It didn't take a brain surgeon to figure out that there was some chemistry happening here. From the nervous, rather idiotic smile on Max's chiseled face to the way his dark eyes darted up and down, drinking in Elizabeth from head to toe, he was clearly quite taken with her. And as for Elizabeth, well, her flushed cheeks combined with the embarrassed yet at the same time curious look in her eyes was a dead giveaway. *We have a love connection,* Vanessa thought. *How charming.*

And how utterly unrealistic!

"Who was that?" Elizabeth whispered as Max traipsed down to the kitchen.

"You haven't figured it out?" Vanessa was incredulous. "You're not half bright then, are you,

Lizzie? It's Max Pennington. Son of the earl. The future Lord Pennington himself."

"He seems much nicer than I expected," Elizabeth remarked as the girls took the final flight of stairs to the fourth floor.

"That's just an act," Vanessa explained. Not that Vanessa had any proof of that. But then again, she'd been here only six months. He still had time to show his true Pennington colors, and Vanessa did not doubt that he would.

"An act? Really?" Skepticism flickered across Elizabeth's features.

Only three seconds of meeting and already she wants to defend him! Vanessa wrinkled her nose in disgust as they made their way down the corridor. "Do yourself a favor, Elizabeth," she warned acidly. "Forget Max. For one, he's what I believe in your country is known as a jerk. I'm afraid they're born that way. For two, he's engaged to be married in six months' time to Lavinia, the duchess of Louster, and trust me, you do not want to cross paths with her. It's their royal wedding we'll be slaving over for the next six months, by the way."

"But he looks so young," Elizabeth replied doubtfully.

"Twenty-one," Vanessa confirmed as they arrived at a small wooden door. "Old enough to get hitched to the witch. Who is herself only nineteen. A child bride by modern standards. Practically on the shelf by British noble tradition." Vanessa took a key from her pocket. "The duchess," she continued, "is, shall we say, a chip off the old ice block. Her father, the earl of Louster—thankfully dead—was a dreadful man and Lord Pennington's best friend. The duke of Louster was feared by all, despised by anyone brave enough to have an opinion. . . ."

Tone it down, Vanessa's inner voice suggested as she continued to enumerate just how hideous Lavinia and her father were. But Vanessa ignored her better instincts. Watching Elizabeth suck it all up and quake in her Reebok sneakers was simply too delicious to pass up. And was this girl ever impressionable!

". . . So I'd stay far from Lavinia if you're at all allergic to snake bites," Vanessa concluded as they entered the bedroom. "And this is our plush suite," she intoned sarcastically. "Bathroom in corner, your bed and closet are to the far left. We share with Alice Henry, who is mostly Mary's help but ours too. Alice is dull as a block of cement and has the IQ of a crustacean, but she minds herself, stays out of the way. Here's your key," Vanessa added, shoving her hand into her pocket and tossing Elizabeth a gold Yale on a rusty ring.

Elizabeth caught it. "Thanks." She looked warily around her and then mustered what Vanessa could see was a brave smile rather than a genuine one. "And thanks for showing me around. And for warning me about witchy Lavinia," Elizabeth joked feebly.

Somehow this annoyed Vanessa. Was Elizabeth going to continue to attempt to chum up to her?

"It's not a joke," Vanessa retorted coldly, "unless you find unemployment funny. Lavinia will have you out on your bum in no time if you don't take her seriously, Elizabeth. And that goes for the rest of these people." She leveled her cold eyes at Elizabeth, who was by this time sitting on her bed, looking somewhat hunched and anxious. "You think Lavinia sounds bad?" Vanessa continued nastily. "Well, she is an angel of mercy compared with Sarah, the earl's spitfire of a daughter. You stay out of her way," she added, "and while you're about it, stay out of mine too!"

With that, Vanessa turned and made for the door. As she turned, she couldn't help the tweak of sympathy that snaked through her insides. Elizabeth really looked the worse for wear. Worn out. Dark circles. Alone. Vanessa knew that feeling only too well.

Too bad, she thought as she turned the brass doorknob, stepped out, and jerked the door shut, hardening herself against any impulse to pop off a kind word to help Elizabeth deal with her first night in the house. But Vanessa wasn't exactly the kind-word type, the warm-welcome type.

She was more of the tough-cookie type.

Yet another thing this Elizabeth Bennet had better learn and learn fast . . . if she knows what's good for her!

What have you gotten yourself into, Elizabeth Wakefield?

Bennet! Elizabeth corrected herself. *It's Elizabeth Bennet now. Elizabeth Wakefield is out of the picture! You didn't want to give your real last name, and you'll have to remember that!*

Her eyes moistened with tears, tears that had been threatening to arrive for over forty-eight hours. Tears she'd managed to swallow back. Until now.

It had all been too much, and Vanessa's chilly presence was the last straw. And so after an evening spent walking miles through her formidably massive new home, Elizabeth lay back on her bed and let the hot salt water run down her cheeks and seep into her hair. Choking back a loud sob, she tried to get ahold of herself, tried to lie still and take deep breaths, but the single cot was somewhat unforgiving. Especially compared with the double futon with extra padding she was used to at home . . .

Home! A feeling of longing washed over her, and Elizabeth's eyes burned. She was absolutely exhausted. She was jet-lagged from the flight to London she'd taken a day earlier and emotionally ravaged by everything that had happened. . . .

Home. Suddenly the word seemed less appealing and luckily far, far away and at least a year ago. Was it really only a day since she'd had such a blowout with her parents in the Chicago airport? Really only a day since she'd hopped a plane for England, bound for her semester abroad on scholarship at the University of London, only to find that she hadn't responded by the deadline and that her place had been given to another student?

Elizabeth half sniffed, half sobbed at the thought of that disappointment. And there was no one to turn to either. For the first time in her life Elizabeth couldn't simply pick up the phone and call a friend, much less a family member. She'd never felt this alone. Totally penniless, she'd ended up riding the tube to her last hope, a youth hostel where she'd hoped to hook up with a friend she'd made at the airport. Pennington House had shone in the distance, and she'd headed over, praying they'd let her spend the night for free. She'd ended up with a job as a kitchen maid, with room and board in addition to a small salary.

But you're lucky, Elizabeth reminded herself as she pushed a tangle of tear-soaked blond hair from her cheek. It was true. The job as kitchen maid was, though unglamorous and hardly what she'd come to England for, nevertheless a lifesaver.

And Elizabeth needed to make it work. It was either that or accept defeat and go home to Sweet Valley. Home to her family. Home to Jessica, who'd forced her to run away in the first place.

At the thought of Jessica a fresh swell of tears rose up through the back of Elizabeth's throat. Finding Jessica, her twin, her best friend, all over Sam Burgess. *My boyfriend!* And they were clearly about to have sex! It had been a total moment of shock for Elizabeth. For one, Sam and Jessica had always hated each other. Yet now they were both prepared to betray Elizabeth for each other?

It was awful. It was ludicrous. It was . . . *over.* Elizabeth shuddered, then forced her mind away from the things that were hurting her. She needed to take a bath and get a good night's sleep. And she needed to keep her thoughts from wandering down paths that only gave her pain.

Think about the positive, she ordered herself, swinging her legs off the bed and ignoring the wave of jet lag that demanded she lie down and

15

sleep for a month. *You're here, and you're Elizabeth Bennet.* And though of course neither of those two things was the most amazing thing to be just now, Elizabeth knew the other options were worse. *After all, who would want to be Elizabeth Wakefield?* Elizabeth asked herself, making herself stand up. *It's not as if that girl had anything going for her!*

Elizabeth winced, but though it hurt, the truth was the truth. Elizabeth Wakefield did indeed have nothing left. Because everything she'd thought she'd had was destroyed in one single moment . . .

Enough of that! Elizabeth walked over to her duffel, unzipped it briskly, and got busy. Unpacking would take her mind off things. It was exactly what she needed. As was this house and this job. No matter how awful, this was a fresh start.

Still. Elizabeth worried as she hung up a sundress. Caustic Vanessa had managed to get under her skin. For someone as pretty and pixielike as Vanessa, it was a shock to see what a sharp tongue she had. Sure, it was obvious the girl was just trying to scare her, but there had to be at least some truth to all the things she was saying. Elizabeth swallowed. No question about it, she had good reason to be fearful. Pennington House's elaborate hierarchy and code of etiquette was as confusing as its floor plan. It was enough to make her brain swirl into total fuzz.

Elizabeth sat down on her bed again and looked out the window onto the manicured lawns that rolled off into the distance, illuminated a silvery gray by a thick band of moonlight. The place was impressive, all right, but also totally formidable. Earls, dukes, duchesses, lords, ladies, maids, maids-in-waiting, house cleaners, housekeepers . . . the nuances and differences were so numerous as to be completely overwhelming, and she felt a headache pinching at her temples. *What kind of world is this?* Certainly not a world she knew, this world of polo clubs and servants' staircases and arranged marriages and people with complicated titles . . .

At that, Max Pennington's handsome face swam into Elizabeth's thoughts. He'd seemed pretty down-to-earth, though. With his Calvin Klein jeans, red polo shirt, bare feet, and sheepish grin, he certainly didn't seem like someone Elizabeth ought to fear. In fact, he'd seemed like just another very cute, very charming guy. A six-foot-two, square-jawed, handsome kind of guy. The kind of guy she wouldn't mind getting to know.

In another world! Elizabeth admonished herself, shooting to her feet and returning to her unpacking. *Here, he's a* sir *to you!*

17

As she placed her one pair of heeled sandals into the back of her closet, Elizabeth forced herself to stick to the facts of her situation. Like Max being out of reach and the pretty shoes: completely useless now. This was a new world with new obligations and new rules. But that didn't mean she had to hate it. After all, the room could have been much worse. Yes, it was fairly spartan, but it was also kind of cozy, and the girls had their own very large, deep, freestanding claw-footed bathtub. Things like that were big pluses in a week of almost total minuses.

And if she didn't like it, Elizabeth knew she had only to revisit her botched attempts to make a life for herself in London. *So much for that!* Elizabeth zipped up her empty duffel and stashed it behind her closet, her jaw clenched in determination as she dismissed a last, fading image of herself busily attending seminars and fiction workshops at the University of London, sipping Twinings English breakfast tea with friends and discussing contemporary British fiction.

But it was time to give up pipe dreams, time to get with the program.

Elizabeth Bennet, scullery maid. This was her life now.

Chapter Two

What a way to start the day! Sixteen-year-old Sarah Pennington groaned inwardly and then suppressed a yawn that threatened to engulf her entire body and turn it inside out. Seven A.M.! The most ungodly hour known to man, and yet here she was, sitting in the office of the Welles School's headmistress. And she was suffering under the beady eye and twitchy, wrinkle-mouthed stare of the Headmonstrous herself—to a sound track of a nasty, ticking grandfather clock that was driving Sarah berserk!

What an outrage! Sarah's stomach churned with anger as she relived the pleasant 5:45 A.M. moment that had gotten her to this less pleasant 7 A.M. moment: She'd snuck her new boyfriend, Nick Jones, into her bed last night, and unfortunately for them, some snitch of a monitor otherwise known as Miss Priss Patricia Mulligan had caught them. Which was bad enough. Even though they weren't doing anything, you'd think they were making a home porno flick from the way the girl had screamed and rushed off to call the authorities. . . .

And now, to go from worse to worst, all hell was about to break loose because not only did Sarah have to deal with the Headmonstrous, but she'd have her father to deal with too. That was the part that made her jittery. The HM she could handle; after all, she was just a minion. But the problem was, the headmistress was also a willing instrument in her father's hands. Right now she looked ready to either flay Sarah or strangle her with Sarah's own long, brown plait—and Sarah had no doubt that one word from her father and the old goat would. That was the power of a title. That was the power of being the earl of Pennington. *And this is the benefit of being his only daughter,* Sarah reflected miserably. *So much for having power over my own life!*

Just then the intercom buzzed, and the goat shot to her hooves. It was her brother, Max, in lieu of the earl, coming to sort things out. Sarah was a little nervy at picturing Max, still rumpled from sleep. He didn't have a hot temper, but he wasn't often roused from his beloved bed before seven either. . . . Still, though Max might be less than thrilled with life, Sarah was also relieved it was only him. At least it wasn't her father. Thank God for the study break that had brought Max home from Oxford, where he was a student. And thank God for the parliamentary sessions that kept the earl out of her hair at times like these.

But Sarah also knew she couldn't stay her father's wrath forever, and she flinched at the thought of his voice booming with anger once he got word of what had happened. Being caught in bed with a boy was bad enough for any sixteen-year-old girl, Sarah knew, but for her it was worse. Always worse. With no mother to soften things and a father who was used to power and control of any and every pleb in his path, Sarah knew she didn't stand much of a chance of leniency.

Oh, to be ordinary. Well, maybe not ordinary, Sarah amended (after all, there are some advantages to being rich and titled), but sometimes being a lady got in the way of being a girl. . . .

"Hello, Miss Hern, it's Max Pennington."

A voice broke into Sarah's daydreams of common life, and she looked up into the familiar, handsome face of her brother, who'd been ushered into the headmistress's office.

Sarah rushed over to greet Max, forcing the old goat to move aside after Max's introduction. "Oh, Max!" Sarah sniffed as she collapsed into her brother's arms, willing her face to crumple and concentrating on getting some tears into her large, blue eyes. "I'm so sorry. This is awful, *just awful!*" she sobbed, clutching Max's jacket.

Sarah felt a bit bad at putting on such a show for her brother, who she adored, but Max was a softie and a sucker for her tears. And he also had the power to keep this incident from her father.

"Sarah, what's going on?" Max demanded, his voice not unkind as he gently loosened her grip on him. "You were in bed with someone?" He shook his head. "Tell me this tabloidal story isn't true."

"Of course it isn't true," she answered hurriedly, her eyes darting nervously to the headmistress, who looked capable of shooting staples with her eyes. "I mean," she amended sulkily, "I did get caught in bed with Nick, but we weren't *doing* anything. We were both fully clothed, for heaven's sake! Please don't tell Daddy, will you?" Sarah beseeched.

"I'm afraid it's too late for that," Miss Hern broke in coldly, her eyes glinting. "I called your father first thing. He instructed me to call your brother to deal with you and bring you home, where he'll be waiting for you. Your father had an emergency meeting this morning and couldn't break away to discuss this . . . situation."

Hell's bells! Sarah swallowed what felt like a

hard-boiled egg in her throat, picturing her father pacing and waiting, a ticking time bomb. Oh, well, there was nothing to do but brace herself for a tidal wave of anger. She'd be sent home for a day of disgrace, and then, like all other times, Sarah knew her father's foul humor would pass and life would go on as normal: *Daddy doing his thing, me doing mine, and never the twain shall meet.* . . .

"I might also add that your father has made his wishes known," Miss Hern continued in a clipped voice, and Sarah looked up. Wishes? What was Heinous Hern talking about now? "He wants you removed," Miss Hern continued in clipped, measured beats, enunciating both syllables of *removed*. "*Re*moved from the boardinghouse, Lady Sarah," she continued acerbically, training her beady eyes on Sarah's face. "From now on, you will be a *day* pupil here at Welles, no longer a boarder."

"*What?*" Sarah exploded in rage, shooting to her feet, her hands clenched into fists. This wasn't happening . . . it couldn't be. "Max?" She looked at her brother, desperately hoping he would contradict Hern, but he nodded. To Sarah it was as if he'd just said yes to a guillotine sentence. Day student? It was unthinkable. She'd have to live at home? At Pennington House? Ugh! All those nosy servants, everyone bustling and scuttling around her . . .

"But I won't have a shred of privacy," she whispered, still disbelieving, to Max. "I won't do it," she added firmly. "It'll ruin my life."

"Too bad, Lady Sarah," Miss Hern broke in swiftly, clearly savoring the bad tidings she'd been allowed to bring. "The decision is final. You must go home at once, please. And your things will be collected tomorrow by your chauffeur."

Sarah began to sob then, really sob, as Max led her to the waiting limousine. And as the limo exited the school grounds for the fifteen-minute car ride home, her sobs turned to wails.

"I'm sorry, Sar," Max mumbled into her hair, giving Sarah a sympathetic squeeze. "But you've really done it this time."

"I didn't *do* anything!" Sarah insisted, anger hot and prickly at her throat. *What will it take?* But there was no use in protesting; she knew that. Max was her older brother. He loved her, but he didn't necessarily understand her. And she told him as much.

"I am sorry for you, truly," Max responded with a sigh as the car drew closer to Pennington House. "I wish I could be a better older sister to a sixteen-year-old. God knows you need a female perspective right now in your life. But I can't help you. I'm a chap," he finished with a lopsided grin, and Sarah punched him lightly on the arm, half

24

annoyed that he'd made her laugh while she was in the middle of a crying jag. "It won't be so bad, though," Max soothed as they neared the giant iron gates with the Pennington crest emblazoned beneath the stone lions on the gateposts. "Look at it this way: Now we'll get to hang out more. It'll be fun."

"Oh, *right*," Sarah muttered snarkily. "Like you'll have time for me with Queen Lavinia around!"

Max protested, but Sarah tuned him out as she stared bleakly at the house rising up in the distance. Now she was truly depressed. Nothing like a view of home on a dark, cloudy day. Especially when your home was a gloomy old stone castle dripping with lichen and you'd been banished to it rather than gone there of your own free will. *That*, Sarah realized, *makes this place a prison!*

Again hot tears sprang to her eyes as the castle loomed closer and closer, dark and forbidding in front of them. Sarah didn't care that inside it was bustling with life and activity. It was still a prison to her.

"Tell me about this guy," Max ventured, leaning forward in his seat. "This Nick. Are you serious about him? You can tell me, you know. Obviously I won't breathe a word of it to the old pater."

Underneath her mournful expression a smile

flickered through Sarah both at the thought of Nick and at the thought of her brother trying to connect with her. Both boys meant so well. But Sarah also knew that though Max had good intentions, he had enough on his own mind and enough of a life to contend with. No matter what Max said, she knew he didn't have time for her. Not when his fiancée was the snottiest, neediest, most demanding, most jealous, most selfish woman in the United Kingdom.

"So you like this chap, I take it?" Max pressed.

"Mind your own beeswax," Sarah responded dismissively, even though inside, her heart was thumping its own answer to Max's question. Was she serious about Nick? *Very serious.* She'd never been more serious about anyone or anything in her life.

The car slowed to a complete stop in front of the castle's main portal doorway, which the family still used. "We're here," Sarah stated, more to herself than to Max.

Here . . . home . . . she sighed heavily. Both words seemed so completely depressing to her. She felt wretched, her legs leaden, not wanting to move. But Sarah also knew she had no choice but to get out of the car. She had to go in and face the music. Even if it was a funeral dirge from the Georgian period.

With a steely, resolute "brave face" Sarah stepped out of the car, her spirits sinking as she stared up at the castle's high, solid walls that for centuries had successfully let no one in and no one out.

Welcome home, Sarah, she thought wryly, took a deep breath, and went in.

"Seven A.M. on the dot!" head housekeeper Mary Dale chirped in a thick cockney accent from the small office to the side of the kitchen. "You're right on time, Elizabeth," Mary added, looking over her spectacles at Elizabeth, who was reporting to the kitchen for her first morning of duty. "Punctuality is certainly an asset, especially when it comes to kitchen work."

Elizabeth stifled a yawn and hoped her shoelaces were tightly tied. She was still jet-lagged, and her head felt kind of waterlogged.

"All right, let's hop to it," Mary said briskly, folding her reading specs away and closing a large ledger marked Invoices. "I'm afraid we've no time for chitchat," Mary continued matter-of-factly, cocking her head and appraising Elizabeth with small, shrewd eyes, her tight gray bun tilting with her head. "There's a lot to go over, so I'll get straight to business."

"Of course." Elizabeth smiled as Mary stood

up from behind her desk, bustled out of the office, and began to outline Elizabeth's kitchen duties.

Elizabeth was impressed. Mary was a large woman, yet she moved quickly. Evidently she was very capable at managing the household. And apparently she'd been there for twenty years . . . *twenty years!* Just thinking of it exhausted Elizabeth. But she forced the thought away. *Look alive!* she commanded herself. There was a lot to take in, and Elizabeth didn't want to look like she wasn't paying attention even for one second. Mary had kind eyes, but it was also clear from her manner that she didn't tolerate laziness of any kind.

"You remember Cook, Matilda Kippers, from last night," Mary said, gesturing toward a woman hovering over a range of hot stoves off to one side of the giant kitchen. "You'll be working for Matilda, doing whatever she needs to get meals planned and prepared."

Matilda nodded at Elizabeth and smiled briefly before getting back to her work. She had a nice, rounded face and very pink cheeks, but her eyes were strained and lined in the corners, and she looked like someone who could snap if pushed. *So stay on her good side,* Elizabeth briefed herself as she moved alongside Mary to "get acquainted" with the pantry.

"Your duties are restricted to the kitchen and

the dining room," Mary stated in her strong, almost Scottish sounding accent as Elizabeth took in the giant, vault-size pantry stocked with mountains of bags and tins. "You will report for the morning shift every morning at seven-thirty A.M., whereupon you and Vanessa will begin laying the table, helping Cook with the food, and otherwise readying yourselves for the family breakfast. Your day ends at six-thirty P.M."

Elizabeth nodded constantly as Mary paraded her through the giant kitchen, reeling off a list of duties and kitchen dos and don'ts. It was rather overwhelming, but Elizabeth gleaned the basic important stuff—that she and Vanessa were to be, as Mary put it, Cook's "right arm and left arm." They would do meal preparation as well as serve the family, clean up, and ensure the kitchen was "spotless" after.

"Sounds like a long day; however, you will have breaks in your schedule as well as an hour for your own lunch," Mary added as she finished walking Elizabeth around the kitchen. "You may do with your breaks as you please."

"But watch you don't go *overtime!*" Matilda cut in, emphasizing *overtime* sharply and staring down into the corner of the kitchen. Elizabeth's eyes followed Matilda's gaze, and she spotted Vanessa trying to scuttle furtively into the kitchen, looking sleepy, her tiny, high-cheekboned face peeping out from underneath her slightly rumpled, cropped pixie hair. "Like Mary said earlier," Matilda barked for Vanessa's benefit, "punctuality is *much* appreciated in this household!"

Elizabeth tried to shoot Vanessa a sympathetic glance, but Vanessa flicked her eyes away and grabbed a pile of buckets from a closet.

"Take a mop and get a bucket from Vanessa, would you, Elizabeth," Mary said, jotting something down in a notebook. "The floor needs mopping."

Definitely no time wasted here, Elizabeth thought as she grabbed a heavy mop and dipped it into a pail full of soapy water. Meanwhile Mary had begun to talk about the finer points of Elizabeth's job, warning Elizabeth to be mindful of etiquette and "most important of all" to "speak *only* when spoken to." It was all quite similar to what Vanessa had said, but definitely not as harsh, although clearly Pennington House had a lot of rules and regulations.

As Elizabeth dragged the mop over the kitchen tiles, she tried to internalize everything Mary was saying, fearful that she might forget an important rule and make an idiot of herself in front of the family. Or worse, lose her job!

"Mind yourself and you'll do just fine, Elizabeth Bennet," Mary concluded her rules lecture, and

Elizabeth winced at the sound of her fake last name. No doubt Mary and the others would not be amused to find out she'd lied about her identity to get hired last night!

Or maybe they'd understand . . . , she thought wistfully. After all, it wasn't like she'd done something wrong that demanded she cover her identity. She was simply trying to start a new life and didn't want her parents or anyone else tracing her. But there was no way of knowing which way someone like Mary might go. *So drop it!*

Elizabeth ducked her head, focusing on the soapy floor in front of her. She wanted to do a good and thorough job and impress Mary. Plus Elizabeth wasn't exactly as experienced a cleaner as she'd made out, and she had a lot of catching up to do. . . .

"Make sure to keep your uniform as clean as possible too," Mary warned, brushing at Elizabeth's khaki pants, where a spot of soapy water had landed. "You should always wear an apron in the kitchen, Elizabeth, but take it off before you go out to serve the family."

Elizabeth nodded. Her head was beginning to get tired of bobbing up and down, but it felt good to stand upright after mopping and walk to fetch an apron from the pegs on the walls. As she put on her apron, Elizabeth glanced down at the uniform and grinned. *At least it's just khaki pants and a blue oxford shirt and not something* from Masterpiece Theater! she reflected, carefully tightening the elastic of her ponytail. Somehow she'd kind of imagined life working for nobility as being straight out of the nineteenth century. But happily Pennington House had rolled with the times, and none of the staff had to wear white frilly caps!

Apparently, though, the Penningtons hadn't exactly shed all their connections to tradition. As Elizabeth mopped, Mary enumerated the seemingly endless, somewhat absurd intricacies of British aristocratic hierarchy and how one ought to apply that knowledge to life at Pennington.

"The earl is to be addressed as Lord Pennington and Sarah as Lady Sarah, but Viscount Maxwell insists on being called simply by his first name, Max, even though he is to be the future earl himself and as the successor to his lordship ought to adopt a more traditional bearing. . . ." Mary prattled away, and Elizabeth simply kept her head at a steady bob while pulling the heavy mop across the floor, her eyes glazing from combined work effort and mental strain as she fought to keep up with Mary's speech. *An earl's wife is a countess, but in English nobility there are no counts, only earls, dukes, and lords . . . ? So where do the counts come from?*

"It may be somewhat difficult for you to

understand the ins and outs of British aristocracy, coming from America and all," Mary observed at a certain point in the conversation.

Am I that obvious? Elizabeth worried. But she had to allow a small nod. After all, it would be pointless to make out that she was fluent in the ways of the British after only a day in their country.

And maybe Mary has more of a point than she even knows, Elizabeth reflected grimly, her back beginning to ache. Not only was Elizabeth from another country, but she was also from another world, a world where everyone was constitutionally equal and therefore seemed full of limitless possibilities. Like Elizabeth, who with her top grades had been made to believe she could be anything she wanted . . .

Elizabeth shuddered as she wrung out dirty water into her bucket, imagining what her parents would say if they could see her now! *From college to cleaning . . . I'm definitely a long way from home!*

Just as she was beginning to feel extremely sorry for herself, Elizabeth was distracted by a loud beeping sound coming from the far end of the kitchen. "The intercom," Mary explained, pressing a button to listen.

"I want a fat-free scone!" an impatient, girlish voice demanded on the other end. "And make it snappy! I'm dying of starvation."

"That's Sarah," Cook explained to Elizabeth. "I wonder what she's doing home at this hour."

"Lady Sarah," Mary corrected. "She likes us to address her with her title. She needs extra attention," Mary added. "Her mother died six years ago, and the teens are troubled years when it comes to our Lady Sarah. She will now be living here at home instead of at her school."

The infamous Lady Sarah, Elizabeth amended. Judging from what Vanessa had to say about her, Elizabeth wasn't wildly keen to meet Sarah—or any of the rest of them—and dreaded lunchtime, when she'd have to meet the whole family with their titles, and special forms of address, and daunting wealth. . . .

But just then Cook smiled at her and asked her if she wanted to help make scones. Obediently Elizabeth wrung out her mop, emptied her pail, washed her hands, and joined Cook in front of a section of the large, rectangular stove.

"Quite simple," Cook said, cracking three eggs into a bowl and handing it to Elizabeth to whisk.

And as she began to whisk the eggs, Elizabeth thought that perhaps Cook might be right about more than just the eggs. Yes, this new job at Pennington House would be grueling in its way, but she had resolved to make the best of it. And she knew she'd make it through if she put her mind to it and focused on the bright side.

After all, if she got to catch glimpses of gorgeous Max and her jobs included serving a couple of scones to a teenager, how bad could it be?

Not bad, Vanessa grudgingly admitted, appraising Elizabeth out of the corner of her eye as the staff drained their cups of tea at the kitchen table. Elizabeth was presently chatting quite animatedly with Davy O'Malley, head gardener. And before that, she'd allowed the seventh servant of the morning, Alice, to get a laugh out of her "Jane Austen" name. Not bad going for someone brand-new at their first Pennington House staff breakfast, surrounded by a bunch of testy British commoners . . . someone from America, no less!

Not that any of this meant Vanessa actually liked Elizabeth. *Not bloody likely.* She still held to her first opinion: Elizabeth was a priss, too earnest, and definitely hiding something. But she could hold her own. She mixed as easily with dingbat (in Vanessa's eyes anyway) Davy as with stern, all-seeing Mary, and you had to respect a girl for that.

"So you're just traveling around indefinitely?" Alice repeated to Elizabeth for the third time, and Vanessa shook her head, annoyed. Alice was about the most dim-witted girl Vanessa had ever known.

35

She needed everything to be repeated a million times. Her mind was like a sieve.

Still, dolts like Alice occasionally came in handy, and Vanessa rather enjoyed the flicker of apprehension crossing Elizabeth's features right about now. Clearly she was keeping something under wraps, and being pestered about her private life was not something she could cope with well.

"Alice, don't be personal," Mary berated Alice, and Alice slunk into her chair, hiding her pimply face under her brown fringe of hair. *Have a little backbone!* Vanessa longed to shout at Alice. The girl was terrified of Mary. *Like everyone else,* Vanessa noted, inwardly snorting with derision. *Everyone except me.* Vanessa wasn't scared of any of these fools, and she had no respect for their tenuous positions of rank. Head housekeeper. Rah rah rah. It was all a load of bollocks. . . .

"Give Elizabeth a hand with the dishes," Matilda said sharply, rapping loudly on the table in front of Vanessa's face. Vanessa scowled and reluctantly got to her feet. By now the rest of the staff had dispersed, leaving only Elizabeth, Vanessa, and Cook—whom Vanessa privately referred to as Matilda the Moron, or Double M for short.

Trying to extend her dawdle time, Vanessa busied herself pretending to get a stain off the kitchen table. She so hated preparing the family breakfast.

It was truly a purgatorial process for her, and with each passing day, it nauseated her even more.

"I've put the bread in the oven, Matilda," Elizabeth reported cheerily from the kitchen. "And I have another batch on the way."

"Good girl," Matilda replied, and Vanessa rolled her eyes. What a goody two-shoes! Elizabeth was darting around the kitchen like a hare on speed, and apart from being thoroughly annoying in its own right, this going above and beyond the call did not bode well for Vanessa! Elizabeth's rapid ascent to servant of the year on her first damned day was only making Vanessa look bad.

But luckily, at least for now, Matilda was so taken up with her elaborate lecture on the topic of which royal ate which kind of egg with which kind of kitchen implement that she wasn't paying attention to Vanessa's work or lack thereof. *Some trade-off, though,* Vanessa thought grimly, sluggishly picking up an empty teacup. The kitchen was unbearable because not only did she have to contend with Busy Lizzie, but she was now being forced to listen to every dreary, mind-numbing detail of Pennington gastronomic history, which Busy Lizzie was lapping up like the eager beaver she was.

Eager beavers, Vanessa ruminated, staring into the empty teacup in her hand. *Eager beavers are not my cup of tea. In fact,* she added, curling her lip in distaste, *come to think of it, serving cups of tea is not my cup of tea!*

Life at PH was definitely getting to be too much for Vanessa, a job so stupefyingly tedious as to be calcifying her every brain cell. And yet she knew she had to grit her teeth and press on. *You're here for a purpose,* she reminded herself, trying to ignore the image of a flushed and hardworking Elizabeth that popped in and out of her frame of vision. *A purpose,* she repeated. *And it's not the paltry Pennington paycheck.*

Vanessa was here for much more than that, and she forced herself to focus on her goals: *You are here for information. You are here for the truth. You need to—*

But Vanessa wasn't even free to finish her thought, for Matilda had let out a shrill beckoning squawk. "Get yourself over here!" she demanded angrily, shoving a silver tray containing a platter of steaming eggs at Vanessa. "We don't have all day to serve breakfast to Max," she added snarkily.

How perceptive of you to note that breakfast isn't an evening affair! Vanessa was dying to sling back, but she bit her lip. It wasn't worth it. Instead she stared into the platter of eggs in front of her, squaring her jaw angrily. As always, her needs had to wait. *Future earl needs eggs,* she thought as she balanced the tray on one hand and surreptitiously polished off half a scone from the table. *Two-minute eggs, to be precise*. Very well. She twisted her mouth contemptuously. She could oblige.

But as she straightened her shirt and took the tray into the dining room, Vanessa kept her mind focused on the future, kept her eyes on the prize. Two-minute eggs for now, but soon the Penningtons would have a lot more on their plates.

Very soon.

Chapter
Three

"I wanted a *chocolate* fat-free scone, not a plain one!" Sarah whined, glaring at Mary, who had come up to her room to retrieve her breakfast tray. "That so-called scone you brought me tasted vile!" *Honestly, is this woman dumb or just deaf?* she wondered, grabbing a brush and yanking it through her light brown hair, which was rippled from the tight plait she'd had it in.

"More tea?" Mary inquired, concern furrowing her brow as she sized Sarah up. But Sarah didn't want Mary's patronizing concern any more than she wanted another infernal cup of bloody tea, which everyone in this house seemed to drink round the clock. *Just because I'm English doesn't mean I'm dotty about tea!* Sarah thought, her eyes flashing with irritation. *And you'd think my own housekeeper would bloody well know it by now!*

"Just go!" Sarah snapped, hurling herself onto her king-size, eighteenth-century four-poster bed. "And draw my bed curtains and window curtains before you leave," she commanded from a sea of down pillows.

As Mary closed the white, spiderweb-thin organza drapes that framed her bed, Sarah lay back on her hand-embroidered silk bedspread and tried to wish herself away by concentrating on the softly moving organza curtains and the music floating through them.

I'm free-floating
On a cloud of me and you . . .

Sarah closed her eyes as her favorite English boy band, U4Me, crooned their latest ballad. *You're my girl, and I'll be true.* The lyrics washed over her, and Sarah felt a longing inside, something pounding at her rib cage.

But something—some*one*—was in the way. "Would you like some—?" Mary began mouthing through the curtains, but Sarah couldn't tolerate the woman for even one more microinstant, and so she held up her remote, thumb pressed firmly on the volume button.

I will never leave you; I am always by your side. . . . But luckily Mary did the opposite and left.

Finally! When she heard the door close behind Mary, Sarah slipped a photograph out from under her school jersey. The photo she'd been mooning over all morning. The photo of the only person other than herself she could think about right now. *Nick* . . .

With his brown-black brooding eyes, olive skin, square jaw, and shoulders you could run a marathon across, Nick Jones was possibly the most drop-dead gorgeous guy Sarah had ever clapped eyes on. And right now, staring into his rugged, handsome face, Sarah felt like she would melt. Even two-dimensional, Nick had the power to make her swoon. She traced his firm jawline as he stared back at her, laughing. He'd given her that picture of him taken outside Piccadilly Circus by some mate or other, and looking at him now, Sarah thought she was lucky to be lying down. Because her legs felt like they'd turned to custard.

Nick was the best thing that had happened to her all year. Maybe even her whole life. Certainly sixteen had been a cruddy year until Nick had shown up. And Sarah had had a massive crush on him for ages. It was only recently that they'd started up, and even then Sarah was worried she might lose him. That's why she'd been a little cavalier this morning, inviting Nick into her bed. She wasn't into doing anything serious, but she was hoping that by showing him a little skin, she'd keep him interested. Because if he lost interest, Sarah thought she might die.

But then of course the hall monitor had nabbed them, and the rest of the day was history. *Like my life,* Sarah thought miserably. Her dad would have her head on a stake for this. . . .

But she wouldn't dwell on all that now. Plenty of time for that when her father returned from Parliament to blast her out until kingdom come!

Adjusting her head on the pillow, Sarah wrapped her arms tightly around the photo of Nick, crushing it against her heart. Everything except Nick felt like hell, and Sarah couldn't ever remember feeling more alone than she had this past year. *Alone . . . why do I feel so alone?* The music mirrored the conflicts in her heart, and Sarah held up the remote and blasted it even louder so that the mournful solo drowned out everything except her own thoughts. Morbid thoughts about being exiled at home with snoopy servants like Mary nosing through her private affairs, watching her like hawks. *Or vultures, which is what they really are—out to get me!*

Sarah shook her head in disgust. For all she knew, Mary was probably being paid extra to spy on her. Sarah wouldn't put it past the old bag, who naturally worshiped the earl and would do anything for him. *If Mum were alive, she'd protect me,* Sarah thought sadly, feeling tears prickle at her eyelids. But her mother had died when she was ten. And Sarah had no one to look out for her. Except of course for Max, but having a caring brother didn't even come close to having a mother.

A tear slipped down the side of Sarah's lightly freckled nose as she thought of her mum. The countess had been the loveliest mum in the world—funny, charming, beautiful, but most of all, warm and real. That's how people described her—as someone who was nothing if not genuine and who didn't care for the meaningless airs and graces that formed the heart of high society.

For her part, Sarah could remember almost everything about her mum, even the way she smelled of magnolia flowers and the fact that she hated strawberries. And of course she would never forget the day that her mum died of cancer. It was the saddest day of Sarah's life.

Oh, Mum . . . Sarah hiccuped. It was times like this that she missed the countess the most, and Sarah felt a familiar hollow burning in her chest. If her mother were here, she'd be able to advise her as to all the confusing feelings roiling around in her heart. Sarah felt sure that with her mother in the picture, she'd feel calmer about day-to-day things, like school and home and Nick. But instead she felt desperate about everything. *It's all looking decidedly pear shaped from here,* Sarah reflected darkly, shoving her face into her pillow. And she felt sure it would only get worse.

As she lay there, Sarah pictured the headmistress of Welles, maybe even at this very moment, having a word with her father. And knowing the old goat, she'd have blown everything out of proportion. Not to mention having told the earl that Nick was on scholarship at Welles and in fact was just a working-class boy from the East End whose sister or mother probably worked as one of the earl's servants, for all they knew. *Working class.* Those were swearwords in her father's eyes. Pure blasphemy.

That's probably why he yanked me out of school! Sarah concluded angrily, sitting up against the headboard, her mouth a thin line. And now she was stuck here, exactly where her father wanted her to be, close to the flock and supervised. *Like a dog on a leash!* she fumed, shaking her head bitterly, the unfairness of it all making her want to bang her head against the wall.

Instead Sarah lay down again and turned her face to the side. Beside her bed, her nightstand fell into her sight lines. On it stood a large, framed picture of Sarah winning the Eaton Winfrey Junior show-jumping competition when she was twelve. Sarah with a happy smile, sitting on her pony, Lightyear. Her dad standing beside them, beaming proudly. Sarah loved that picture, and she picked it up and stared at it sadly. *Dad* . . . he looked so sweet there. Just like an ordinary dad.

Sarah loved her father, but she also recognized how much they'd grown apart. He just didn't understand her anymore. *He thinks I'm still that little girl,* Sarah mused, gazing at the photograph. But she wasn't. She'd outgrown her pony and was now into boys. *That's* normal, *for God's sake!*

But her father wanted her to save herself until she was eighteen, at least, and marriageable. To someone eligible, of course, like James Leer, her brother's best friend. *Please! Like he'd even look at me!* Sarah shook her head in annoyance. James was hot and all, but her father simply didn't live in the real world. In the real world James was no more interested in Sarah than in flying to the moon. Especially since he was all gaga over the sourpuss scullery maid, Vanessa, who—weirdly enough—wasn't even faintly interested, despite her lowly station. *The girl's about as soft as a bed of nails!*

Sarah rolled her eyes and sighed loudly. This whole love thing was just too confusing. Like why would someone as low-level as Vanessa have no interest in a gorgeous rich guy like James? Admittedly, Vanessa was gorgeous enough to attract many men, but she was also just a maid and therefore, in Sarah's eyes, could hardly afford to be picky. It was odd. Like love itself.

Love is what I need; it's an addiction to me. . . . Lifting her wrist, Sarah abruptly switched CDs with her remote. She'd had her fill of love songs for the day. She needed something loud and brash to dull her mind and help her pass the time. She still had hours to go before she'd see Nick again. She'd promised to meet him outside the school at four. *Which might be a little tough to pull off now,* Sarah admitted bitterly. Now that she was in this gloomy castle, this fortress crawling with her father's army of serfs . . .

Abruptly Sarah hopped out of bed and began pacing the length of her suite. Thinking about fortresses and prisons made her feet itchy. She simply had to get out of there, or she'd go mad.

Pausing at the window, Sarah stared glumly out, across the turrets marking a cupola rising off the third wing, across the expansive gravel driveway, across green lawns that gave rise to high, lichen-covered stone walls.

Wish we had a moat—so I could drown myself in it! Everything else around her—including her father—seemed like it was from the Middle Ages. *So why not a moat?* Sarah pondered angrily. No question, in her mind: The family badly needed to modernize in many more ways than one. For starters, moving out of this damp dump to a posh pad in Central London. And, of course, staying out of their children's personal lives!

Wishful thinking! Frustration prickled her skin, and Sarah angrily turned away from the hated view beyond the window and padded across her Persian rug to her laptop. At least, if nothing else, she could send SOS e-mails, Sarah consoled herself, typing her best friend Victoria's address into the mail window.

Dear Vixen, she began, and then stopped. She always liked to title her e-mails before she got started. And this one would be easy: *Hard Times,* Sarah typed into the title line, scowling as she stared at the computer screen, wishing she could live anywhere but here, wishing she were anyone but herself. . . .

This is nice. . . . Elizabeth hummed as she stepped out of the kitchen's back door and turned down a narrow, cobbled path lined on either side with foxgloves and snapdragons. After a bad start it had shaped up to be a perfect morning—unusual for English weather, she'd been told. The sky was a robin's-egg blue, and the perfectly trimmed lawns shone an almost emerald green as Elizabeth made her way to the herbarium, where she'd been sent to collect fresh greens for the family lunch. *Not a bad job,* she reflected with a contented smile as she breathed in the scent of fresh lavender and honeysuckle drifting on a light, warm breeze.

If things continued in this vein, Elizabeth thought she might have to admit to actually *liking* being a scullery maid! And as she wandered down the pleasantly winding stone path, admiring the flower gardens around her, Elizabeth concluded that life so far at Pennington House was really not half as bad as she'd anticipated. Sure, the work was hard, but it was also mindless. And the staff were nice. *Except for Vanessa,* Elizabeth amended. But Elizabeth also theorized that it wouldn't take too long before Vanessa would give up her I'm-more-abrasive-than-a-pot-scourer act and come around.

"Wow," Elizabeth whispered in amazement as she took in the sight of the sinuous curves of sloping green lawn unfolding below her. Not a single blade of grass was out of alignment. And at the bottom of the hill there was even a real English maze! The closest Elizabeth had ever come to seeing one of those was when she'd rented *The Shining*!

As Elizabeth surveyed the gardens in front of her—the razor-backed topiary hedges of the maze just begging to be explored—she had to fight off the urge to loosen her tight ponytail, tumble down the inviting hill, and amuse herself in the maze. But she couldn't. She had a chore to finish.

If she could find the herb garden.

Mary said it was just beyond the fountain. . . .
Elizabeth frowned in confusion as she retraced her
steps back to the fountain she'd passed—an impressive marble spout with a mermaid nestled at
the base, surrounded by lilies. But there was no
herb garden in sight.

"We must stop meeting like this!"

Startled, Elizabeth looked up to see Max ap-
proaching, a joking smile on his face. Elizabeth felt
a slight flush form and managed—she hoped—to
control it. Max looked really great, his lean body
accentuated by a pair of loose cargo pants and a
white Oxford University T-shirt with a huge hole
in the side. Suddenly Elizabeth felt self-conscious
in her PH uniform. The khaki pants seemed somehow dorky with the belt they had to wear, and her
hair felt too scraped back in her ponytail.

"I'm afraid I'm a bit lost," Elizabeth replied,
worrying suddenly if she was on forbidden turf.
She still hadn't wrapped her head around all the
don'ts in the servants' rules—she was still busy
working on getting the dos right!

But Max seemed unfazed, so Elizabeth relaxed.
"Wrong fountain," he explained, directing her to
the herbarium. "And it's a left out of the kitchen
back door. You took a right."

"Still jet-lagged, I guess," Elizabeth replied
with a sheepish shrug. "Um, thank you . . . sir,"

she breathed, a scissor of fear snaking through her insides as she took in Max's frown. *Isn't he to be addressed as Master Max? Or maybe Viscount?*

"Oh, please, it's just Max. Nothing fancy for me," Max said, looking embarrassed and running a hand through his shaggy, almost black hair. "And you are . . . ?" he added with what seemed to Elizabeth to be kind of a shy smile.

"Elizabeth . . . Bennet."

"Right," Max replied, his shy smile widening. "An unforgettable name," he added. "Lovely to meet you, Elizabeth."

Elizabeth's heart began to hammer in her chest as Max held her gaze. He really was very good-looking. By anyone's standards. And more than that, he radiated kindness and a sort of unstudied, low-key gracefulness . . .

Max looked away, and Elizabeth felt embarrassed to still be standing there, staring at him, practically openmouthed as a guppy. "Thanks," she muttered quickly, and headed down the path to the herbarium. *You'd better get moving too,* she chastised herself as she glanced at her watch. Cook would be getting anxious by now!

Alone at last! Vanessa crept quietly along the main corridor of the right wing of the house's second floor. Although she knew no one was around—Lord P.

himself was still safely stashed in Parliament—she kept her movements stealthy and quiet as she headed for his suite. No need to make any undue noises that might catch the attention of nosy parkers like Mary. Or that brat, Sarah—though judging from the music Vanessa could hear through even these thick castle walls, Sarah was doubtless still moping around in her suite, making Greek tragedy out of her piffling problems.

Vanessa's eyes narrowed in determination as she quickly slid the key she'd copied from Mary's master set into the keyhole of the earl's suite. She tried not to be impatient as she jiggled it, but she knew she didn't have that much more time. Her break was almost over, and the dreaded lunch shift was almost in session. But she had to get in.

Bingo! The lock clicked, and Vanessa swung open the heavy door and slipped her slender frame around the door, closing it softly behind her. The room waited, a vast monument to all things noble and over-the-top—rococo antique bed, stuffed leather chairs, stiff chintz drapes heavy enough to sink a ship. The sort of rich-snob useless extravagance that Vanessa loathed.

"Ow! Bloody ottoman!" she swore viciously under her breath, rubbing her shin where the offending and offensive orange block had banged into her. Ottomans. Exactly the kind of furniture that said it all to Vanessa. Who used them? What

53

was their function? They had no function, as far as she was concerned. They were as outdated and silly and oafish and absurd as nobility itself!

But Vanessa kept her swearing to a minimum. She truly did not want Mary to catch her, and the old woman had the ears of a thoroughbred hunting dog. If she were caught, Vanessa knew she'd be fired on the spot, which—though a lovely thought in and of itself—would defeat the purpose of why she'd come to Pennington House in the first place.

Instantly Vanessa's mouth softened into something resembling sadness. Sadness shot through with anger. After a bitter childhood with her tormented, alcoholic-depressive excuse for a mother, Vanessa had wanted nothing more than to escape her roots and disappear into the city of London, where she could start afresh.

But then her mother had died, and Vanessa had discovered among her possessions a letter that would change everything. A letter addressed to the earl of Pennington and postmarked eighteen years ago. Vanessa could recall every sentence of it. Until the letter, she'd thought her mother had gin running through her veins instead of blood. She'd never seemed to care about anyone, least of all herself. But then Vanessa saw the feeling and emotions in the letter and realized her mother had once been someone with hopes and dreams of her own.

I am pregnant with our child, darling. . . . I know it will come as a surprise. . . . But I love you and hope we can be a family for our baby. . . .

Vanessa's pale skin felt like it had been stretched too tight across her cheekbones as she thought of her mother's trembling, spidery handwriting, so filled with hope and love.

Except that the letter was marked Return to Sender and unopened. And it had lain among her mother's things ever since.

Until now. Vanessa hardened her expression and moved steadily through the earl's bedroom, gazing at all the finery spread out in front of her. She laid her hands on the earl's polished antique oak bureau, his solid-silver comb glinting next to her hand.

Vanessa gripped the top drawer, her face a mask as she pulled it open and began to methodically rummage through the contents.

Vanessa's mother had always joked that Vanessa was the secret child of the "earl of P.," but since she was always drunk, Vanessa had never taken any notice. All along she'd believed her mother was just a tart and a lush, going through men like she went through bottles of liquor. But underneath, Vanessa knew now, there had been a woman in pain. A woman who'd once had self-respect and dreams of a family life.

Except that the earl had never acknowledged her or Vanessa, and Vanessa's mother had been forced to raise a child alone, with no money or child support.

With nothing.

Angrily Vanessa slid the bureau drawers closed and headed for the earl's closet. She was convinced that somewhere there had to be proof of her mother's affair with Lord Pennington. A letter, a photograph, a journal, something. Either here or in the countess's suite. Her wing had been closed off and off-limits to everyone for six years, but Vanessa had a key to it, had already done a preliminary search a week earlier, and planned on returning and next time ransacking it from top to bottom.

She slid her hands through the earl's rack of silk ties. She unhinged hatboxes. She inspected everything. She even removed the shoehorns from the earl's shoes. Nothing. But Vanessa wasn't giving up yet. Not ever. The only reason she'd come to work at the house was for revenge. And she would have it if it killed her.

You'll pay, Vanessa vowed, thinking of her brokenhearted, penniless, pregnant mother as she headed to the earl's nightstand. On top of it, his gold pinkie ring with the Pennington crest sat in a small gold dish. She touched the ring, and a shiver of revulsion pulsed through her. She didn't want Lord Pennington's family name. Or his money. Or any of the material vestiges of power that he and his stupid family were so proud of. All Vanessa wanted was to make the earl suffer. And his children. She would take her mother's secret and shove it in their well-bred faces.

But first she needed proof.

"Dammit!" Vanessa swore softly under her breath as she heard the unmistakable purr of the earl's Rolls-Royce, the crunch of its tires on gravel. He was home. She had to get out of there.

Swiftly Vanessa put the earl's suite to rights, her heart knocking at her rib cage as she heard him bustling through the front door down below.

Time was running out, but she had yet to get out of the room!

With a last look around, Vanessa darted out of the suite and jammed the key into the old lock.

Just in time.

The earl came up the stairs just as Vanessa shot behind a curtain in the corridor, thanking her mother's genes for her slim frame, which slipped easily behind the folds of the heavy drape.

Peeping through a fold in the fabric, Vanessa made out the form of the earl, his slightly portly stomach and broad shoulders in a tweed suit. His face was tired and sagging, she was pleased to note.

But he didn't look nearly as awful as he would when, before long, Vanessa came to him with the proof she knew she would find and ruined his reputation in one memorable moment.

Watch out . . . Dad, she mouthed silently as she watched the earl enter his suite.

Lord Pennington had wrecked her mother's life. Now Vanessa would wreck his.

"Yes, Dad?" Max Pennington inquired, popping his head around the door of the earl's suite to see his father changing from shoes to a pair of old red velvet slippers. The earl had just intercommed that he'd like to see Max.

"Come in, Max," Lord Pennington replied with a tired smile. "Awfully long parliamentary session this morning. And I couldn't really concentrate," he added, his broad brow furrowing in concern. "I'm too worried about Sarah."

"Well, you'll be pleased to know she's home, then," Max replied, seating himself in a leather armchair. "She's in her room," he added. "And she's very sorry." Max knew his father wouldn't believe that for a second, but he had to throw it in for Sarah's sake.

"Good." The earl sighed as he removed his tweed jacket and hung it on a wooden hanger. "I'm pleased to hear that the situation is contained. But I will give Sarah a severe talking-to after lunch," he added sternly. "This is no trifling matter."

"I understand Dad, but—," Max began, leaning forward in his chair as his father looked at him blankly. Max swallowed. He had to pick his words carefully. He didn't want to stoke the fire and anger his father more than he already was. *And of course he has a right to be,* Max acknowledged. At the same time Max knew that his father had a tendency to overreact. Especially when it came to Sarah, his only daughter.

"What is it?" the earl prompted somewhat impatiently as he pulled a thick Aran sweater over his head.

"I just thought that maybe you should go easy on Sarah," Max replied boldly. The earl frowned and was about to open his mouth. "I'm not trying to excuse Sarah's behavior," Max continued evenly. "Not one iota. Of course you were right to punish her, but Dad, remember that she's just a teenager."

"That's no excuse," the earl responded swiftly, fixing Max with his piercing blue eyes. "Sarah needs to learn her lesson. She must learn that fraternizing beneath one's station is simply not done!" the earl continued crossly. "Not to mention getting caught in bed with *anyone,* nobleman or commoner," he added, his eyes flashing beneath white eyebrows knitted together with a mixture of anxiety and anger. "Quite frightful, really!"

"Yes, Dad. Of course, sir," Max mumbled, feeling defeated as he stood up from the chair and took in his father's continued mutterings about Sarah's shocking behavior, and class, and stations. . . .

"It's just not done," the earl repeated. "One must know one's place in society!"

Max nodded, which he knew from experience was all he could do when his father got onto this track, but inside he felt a tremor of something passing through him. He couldn't quite identify the tremor, but it had something to do with feeling weary of tradition, which he'd always found more tedious than he could ever say, and something about the ridiculousness and arbitrary nature of what was "done" and "not done," the sort of thing his fiancée, Lavinia, was always harping on about, the sort of thing that so often seemed like meaningless babble to Max.

And it also had something to do with Elizabeth. An image of the new American scullery maid flashed very quickly in front of Max's eyes. He didn't know the first thing about her, but he did know that she had the thickest milk blond hair he'd ever seen. And a warm, generous smile.

So much warmer than Lavinia's . . .

Chapter Four

What a bloody waste of time! Vanessa fumed silently as she scuttled into the kitchen. To have spent her break in the earl's suite and come away completely empty-handed for her efforts . . . nothing could anger her more!

But now was not the time to show it.

Vanessa fingered the key to the earl's suite in her pocket as she eyed the key rack, where Mary's master set was suspended. Vanessa had made a copy of the necessary keys when she'd first arrived, but she liked knowing the master set was there, just in case. Making copies had been smart. Otherwise, she'd have to sneak the keys off the rack.

Not that she was too worried about being caught. As usual these days, Mary was ensconced in her off-kitchen office, thoroughly engrossed in conversation with the head gardener, Davy. They were discussing Max's wedding. *The bloody royal wedding, from the way they're carrying on!* Vanessa mused in annoyance, rolling her eyes as Mary and Davy continued their urgent chatter. They were carrying on about the fact that the wedding was "only" six months away! As if six whole months of preparation weren't trouble enough!

"I did put a set of roll-on lawn into the garden's northern hill this morning, just to see how the color looks," Davy apprised Mary. "And we're okay on pruning . . . now I just need the earl's say-so on the plans for our new shrub and flower plantings, and then we can initiate that operation," Davy jabbered on self-importantly.

It was all Vanessa could do not to yell out in disgust. Even the hired help around here thought they were something just because they worked for the earl. Davy, for instance, clearly thought his "operation" was of grand-scale global importance on a par with the launching of the *Mir* satellite or the release of Nelson Mandela. *Take a reality pill.* Vanessa snorted, unable to contain her irritation. *You're pushing a few petals around, that's all!*

"Something wrong with your legs, Vanessa?" Mary snapped, shooting her a cold glare. Evidently she'd overheard Vanessa's snort because she looked decidedly unimpressed. "Get a move on," she added impatiently. "The lunch buffet needs arranging, and Cook needs you to get hot platters out of the oven!"

"I'm coming," Vanessa replied sulkily, pulling on her apron and moving over to the island, where Cook stood slaving over the giant slab of iron stove, her mouth souring into a prune shape as Vanessa came near, even though Vanessa had done nothing wrong and wasn't even late! *What a pill!* Vanessa reflected, glaring at Matilda's broad back, wishing that looks could really kill—or at least maim. Cook was such an irritating person, totally ruled by the earl's chief lackey, Mary. If Mary was annoyed with Vanessa, Cook would always follow suit. The woman couldn't even think for herself!

And as if things weren't bad enough, Vanessa also had to endure Elizabeth's overzealous scurrying about. She had already removed a large dish of lasagna from the oven and was busily arranging Italian parsley on the dishes as if her life depended on it. Plus the family silver had already evidently been polished. Platters and serving spoons gleamed from the counters, arranged in neat, perfect lines.

Garnish this! Vanessa scowled at Elizabeth, whose perky features, flushed from hard work, grated Vanessa's nerves only slightly less than Elizabeth's service-with-a-smile expression.

Beeep. Beep-beep! The intercom hummed impatiently. It could be one person and one person only.

"I'm starting a low-fat diet!" Sarah intoned through the loudspeaker. "Make sure I have a fruit cup and a green salad without olives or cheese or protein of any kind!" she commanded.

Elizabeth chuckled as she placed crockery on the silver serving trays. "An hour ago she intercommed through that she wanted to start a high-protein diet," Elizabeth informed Vanessa with a giggle.

As if I care! Vanessa slapped a pat of butter onto an embossed silver butter dish, her cheeks reddening from annoyance. Sometimes she didn't think she would be able to tolerate even one more minute of this joke for a job, let alone another month!

But she knew she had to stick it out. *Whatever it takes,* she vowed as Elizabeth continued to patter on about Lady Sarah's "humorous" whims.

Vanessa didn't find them humorous at all. They appalled her. They were simply more evidence of how spoiled and self-centered the earl's bratty daughter could be.

But Vanessa *could* smile at the thought of the day the brat's mouth would drop open like a trapdoor. The day she would find out that the lowly kitchen help she had ordered around for so long was none other than her own half sister and her father was nothing but a philandering, low-caliber sleazebag.

That was something Vanessa could smile about. Indeed.

Here goes! Elizabeth swallowed nervously as she picked up the silver coffeepot, which she'd just refilled, smoothed her hair with her free hand, and entered the dining room.

Aside from Max, she hadn't met the family yet. Vanessa had served during lunch while Elizabeth helped Cook with preparations and scrubbed dirty pans. But now it was 1:30 P.M., and Vanessa had opted out of serving the earl his second cup of coffee.

"You go," she'd said sullenly to Elizabeth. "I've had enough for one mealtime."

Elizabeth glanced at the earl and Sarah, careful not to seem impudent or staring. The earl was smaller than she'd imagined and didn't look remotely like the evil, oafish ogre Vanessa had made him out to be. In fact, with his newspaper and his reading glasses, he looked pretty much like any other dad reading the paper after lunch.

"Thank you," the earl said as Elizabeth carefully refilled his china coffee cup. "You're new, aren't you?" he added, looking at Elizabeth from over the wire rim of his glasses.

"Yes, Lord Pennington," Elizabeth replied smoothly, pleased that she'd remembered the correct mode of address and pleased and surprised that the earl had noticed her.

"Welcome to Pennington House, then," the earl remarked kindly. "And what's your name?"

"Elizabeth Bennet." Elizabeth smiled at the earl as she poured cream from a tiny pitcher on her tray. *Definitely not an ogre,* she thought. Of course, she'd known before that Vanessa had exaggerated in her descriptions, but now it seemed she'd basically gone and made everything up.

"Elizabeth *Bennet?*" Sarah exclaimed, picking at a salad with her fingers. "Like from *Pride and Prejudice?*" she asked incredulously.

"Yes . . . Lady Sarah," Elizabeth replied, feeling stiff and uncomfortable at addressing a sixteen-year-old so formally.

"We're reading that book at school," Sarah replied, and then yawned loudly. "It's *utterly* boring," she finished, her eyes flickering over Elizabeth with a look as if to indicate that she, Elizabeth, was personally responsible for Jane Austen's novel.

Maybe Vanessa wasn't lying about everything, Elizabeth amended silently. Sarah certainly did seem to be a handful. She was pretty in a well-bred, even-featured way, but her small, heart-shaped face looked dissatisfied and pinched, and her blue eyes roved moodily around the room as if being at the table for lunch was torture.

"Put your hand in front of your mouth when you yawn," the earl reprimanded Sarah sharply, rattling his newspaper.

"I'm just so bored!" Sarah shot back, snatching at an éclair on Max's plate and dusting her pale lemon cashmere cardigan with icing sugar in the process. "I wish someone else were eating with us. It's so dull when it's just us," she whined, brushing at her sleeve and shaking her head in annoyance as Elizabeth ventured toward her with the coffeepot. "It's just milk in my coffee cup. I *hate* coffee," she added, clearly annoyed that Elizabeth had even offered.

"Your prayers will be answered soon, Sarah." Max spoke up cheerfully. "I've invited James for dinner tomorrow night."

Elizabeth noted a gleam of interest in the earl's eye as he took in the news of Max's friend's arrival. "Splendid idea," the earl responded, looking at Sarah. "Be sure you act like the lady that you are, Sarah," he cautioned her while she rolled her eyes. "James is not the sort of chap to enjoy dining with a girl who yawns at the table!"

Elizabeth couldn't help a small smile at this display. For all their wealth and titles, the Penningtons seemed just like any other family, parents sparring with the children and telling them to mind their table manners. This was comforting to Elizabeth. *I may just end up liking them,* she mused contentedly as she began to clear the dessert buffet.

"James Leer is a friend of mine, Elizabeth," Max said suddenly. "He lives on the estate adjacent to ours. And he just got back from New York."

"Oh," Elizabeth replied, startled but not displeased that Max was engaging her in conversation, though she'd steered clear of looking at him much up until now, partly out of shyness and partly because she was afraid it would be rude. *Perhaps Vanessa really was playing me!* Elizabeth considered as Max began drawing her into a conversation about the United States, asking her questions about her hometown. Perhaps this was how things really were at Pennington House, with servants interacting pleasantly with the family, not fearing for their lives!

Talking to Max was easy, and between stacking empty dishes Elizabeth found herself answering Max's questions quite naturally and unselfconsciously, despite the fact that she didn't want to give away too much about her background.

". . . So I just thought it would be fun to take some time off during college," Elizabeth explained in answer to Max's questions about how she came to be at Pennington. "And I thought it might be fun to come and work in England. Get to experience what it's like to live in the country by working a job like this," she finished cheerily as Max nodded, his eyes lively and interested.

Just then the earl coughed loudly, rattled his paper, and fixed Elizabeth with a rather stern look. "That'll be *all*, Elizabeth," Lord Pennington announced loudly.

Elizabeth felt her face turn redder than the beet salad she'd laid out for the family buffet. She'd overstepped the mark and been put in her place! The earl had dismissed her!

It was all so embarrassing.

Especially in front of Max.

Lowering her eyes, Elizabeth slipped out of the dining room, eager to get as far from the family as possible, shame burning through her face as she realized how silly she'd been to think that the Penningtons were an ordinary family. They weren't ordinary at all. They might seem ordinary on the outside, but they were blue bloods. And this was England, not America. Class was everything. *And you're the lowest,* Elizabeth reminded herself. *So stay down!*

This is ludicrous! Sarah's features blackened into a scowl as she stomped down the hallway toward her father's study. Trust her father to summon her to his study for their little "talk" instead of somewhere more neutral. But this way he could loom over his giant mahogany desk at her, seething with disapproval while she quaked in her chair like some lowly subject! That was evidently his plan.

Steeling her face into a tight, defiant mask, Sarah resolved to act anything but apologetic in front of her father as she entered his office and slouched angrily into an armchair across from the earl, who was pacing up and down the length of his study.

Of course, for his part, the earl looked like he'd just swallowed a wedge of lemon. He'd looked like that all through lunch, though of course during the meal he hadn't said a word about the "incident" to Sarah, simply made cutting remarks about her table manners! *Typical!*

Sarah leveled her gaze at her father, keeping her eyes unwavering, though a tremor of fear skittered up her spine. Her father did have a tremendous temper, and having kept it bottled up all through lunch only meant his wrath would be doubly severe now that he could let it all out.

But I will not apologize! Sarah told herself, knowing that an apology would help her situation but knowing also that she had to stand her ground in front of her father. Why should she apologize?

If anyone was owed an apology, it was Sarah. For being ripped out of school and away from her friends. For having to suffer through life as the child of a fuddy-duddy father whose value system identically matched that of the Victorians.

"If I were you, I would wipe that scowl off my face," the earl began in a voice already vibrating with anger. "Your appalling behavior this morning is bad enough. A little contrition would only serve to better your case, my girl!"

Contrition! Sarah mashed her lips together to keep from shouting the word back in her father's face! There was no way in hell that she'd act contrite right now, and she didn't give a hoot whether it would "serve her case" or not. As far as she was concerned, she was damned already—but she wasn't about to beg for mercy!

"Your behavior is bad enough on its own terms," the earl continued, lacing his hands behind his back and pacing angrily back and forth from one bookcase to another. "It's bad enough getting caught in the same bed with a boy but worse because of who you are, Sarah, and with whom you choose to consort!"

"What's that supposed to mean?" Sarah shot back bitterly, and then wished she'd taken it back. The earl's face was seething with anger now, and though Sarah might be filled with a self-righteous

71

indignation of her own, she wasn't immune to her father's anger. If only Max were there to act as a buffer . . . but Sarah knew she had to sit in the hot seat alone and endure the tirade, which appeared to be in full swing now.

"To be caught in bed with this—this *Nicholas*," the earl sputtered angrily. "This Nicholas, whoever he is! Sarah, you are not a commoner, and you should know better!"

"You can't tell me who to go out with!" Sarah snapped back, her eyes glittering a bright blue with angry tears.

"I'm afraid I can, and I shall!" the earl boomed. "This young man is *inappropriate* for a girl of your station. And your actions reverberate," the earl continued, glaring at Sarah from beneath his disapproving white eyebrows. "You have embarrassed the family name. Not to mention the other . . . ramifications." The earl coughed a little but pressed on. "We all know what can happen to girls who make poor judgment calls."

"And I find your butting in on my affairs *inappropriate*," Sarah burst out, her cheeks blazing with anger. "And we all know what can happen to fathers who—"

"That is enough! Be quiet, young lady!" The earl held up a warning finger, and Sarah glared at it, fuming with humiliation and resentment. "This is the bottom line, Sarah," her father continued in a more normal tone of voice. "I forbid you to see this Nicholas . . . Jones. And if you don't behave, I'll be forced to home school you."

"What?" Sarah couldn't believe what she was hearing. It was so medieval as to be positively abusive. "Forbid me to see Nick? Home school me if I don't obey you?" she hissed. "You can't do that."

"I can, and I will," the earl replied calmly, seating himself in his chair. "I'm sorry, Sarah, but you've forced my hand with this Nicholas character. And as for home schooling, well, it's your choice. Follow my rules and you'll have some semblance of a normal social life. Disobey and you'll be completely isolated here at Pennington, with tutors instead of teachers. It's up to you!"

No Nick, no social life, what else is there? Sarah quivered with horror. Of course she'd expected her father to officially disallow her seeing Nick, but the threat of home school was a scary surprise.

"Are we perfectly clear?" the earl asked in a stern, even voice.

No, we're not! You have no right to rule my life! Sarah wanted to scream, but she bit her lip hard instead, almost to the point of breaking the skin. She knew her father was serious. And she knew if she wasn't careful, she'd end up like Rapunzel, stuck in her room, hidden from the world. *Hidden from Nick!* It was a dreadful notion, but Sarah knew her father would have no qualms about going through with his threat to keep her imprisoned at Pennington. No, there was only one thing to do: tread carefully.

Because if there was one thing Sarah could depend on, it was her father's will. And when he said he would do something—good or bad—he always did it. He was a man of his word.

"I said, are we perfectly clear?" the earl repeated in a threatening tone.

"Crystal," Sarah muttered, keeping her eyes on the floor. She didn't even want to look at her father, he was making her so violently, hatefully angry. Plus she wanted the sermon to be over with as quickly as possible. She had to get out of there and do some planning.

"Good." The earl tried to smile. "Now, let's just try to move on, shall we, love?" he began in a conciliatory tone, but Sarah tuned him out, though she bobbed her head a few times, pretending to listen. But Sarah couldn't care less for this part of the chat. Her head was too full of anger, which she was trying to shut out by thinking of Nick and wondering how she could get a chauffeur and get back to school. She'd arranged to meet Nick behind some rosebushes at 4 P.M., and it was an appointment she intended fully to keep.

After all, like her father, when Sarah said she would do something—good or bad—she always did it.

She was a girl of her word.

"Your slovenliness is catching up with you, it is," Cook ranted, shaking a plump finger at Vanessa. "You've been very lackadaisical about your duties of late, and I am not pleased; I'm not. Not at all."

Oh, please! Vanessa kept her face expressionless and her eyes neutral, but she was dying to swat the woman. Matilda's mouth, when open, was a constant stream of nonsense. And all the sorts of cutesy country English turns of phrase that people expected from servants, Matilda delivered. She was a walking, talking character straight off a Merchant-Ivory film set.

And she was also driving Vanessa up the wall.

"Elizabeth has been here only one day, and already she's got this kitchen into tiptop shape," Matilda continued, launching into yet another eternal bleating about Vanessa's flaws in attitude, skill, and "general ways," whatever the dickens that was!

I never promised you a picnic, Vanessa responded

silently, fantasizing that chunky Matilda had a plug somewhere on her bulk, which Vanessa could open, thus deflating the woman. Or perhaps with a good yank she could rise like a helium balloon and live up near the high ceiling, where she could squeak away until dolphins reclaimed the Thames.

"You dropped two plates already today, you did," Matilda babbled on. "And your slowness! Vanessa, you move with the speed of a reptile!"

Vanessa had to work hard to suppress a loud guffaw at that one and settled on a slight smirk instead. The speed of a reptile. *Why, thank you!* she wanted to say, but she knew Matilda was too thick to appreciate that she'd just paid Vanessa an inadvertent compliment. Clearly the woman was too idiotic to know that crocodiles and alligators and lizards and all manner of reptiles moved like lightning.

And as if the situation weren't low-level enough, Vanessa could see—despite the glazing over of her eyes—Elizabeth the Perfect beetling away in the corner, expertly and energetically wiping down the countertops.

And then to cap it all off, there was Mary Dale, looking on from her office and nodding appreciatively at Cook, sanctioning the dressing-down of Vanessa, which clearly gave the women much joy.

Spare me! Vanessa shot Cook a withering look and folded her thin, lightly muscled arms contemptuously. The scene was getting even more pathetically stereotypical, Vanessa noted, as Cook had switched from the wagging finger to the wielding of her wooden spoon. Oh, it was all too much!

Vanessa gritted her teeth, wondering seriously how much longer she'd manage to endure the company of such utterly moronic and asinine people. The work was punishment enough, but the people she had to deal with really took the cake, as far as she was concerned. Even the so-called well-meaning ones, like Mary's helper Alice.

Hang in there! Alice seemed to say as she shot Vanessa a sympathetic smile from the pantry, where she was taking inventory. Alice was a stringy, rather sorry-looking girl, and not the brightest bulb in the chandelier either. And if anyone knew what it was like to be lectured at, it was Alice, who had lately been getting into loads of trouble with Mary.

But Vanessa didn't need Alice's sympathy and flicked her eyes away. She didn't need sympathy. She didn't need lectures either. All she needed was to be left alone.

Proof. I need proof, Vanessa mused as Matilda went into the closing remarks of her speech, à la,

"You are toeing a fine line, you are!" *Proof* . . . of the earl's "indiscretion." *That's probably what he'd call it!* Vanessa reflected bitterly.

And she needed that proof soon. Because if she had to suffer through much more of life at Pennington House, Vanessa felt sure she might go quite mad and end up slitting her wrists with Cook's carving knife!

Chapter
Five

"Good show!" Lord Pennington panted as Max deftly maneuvered his stallion in front of the earl's, hooked his father's mallet, and swiped the ball away from him.

"Thank God the chukker's over." The earl groaned as the umpire signaled the end of the polo set. Max, too, was grateful for the break. Though each set, or chukker, lasted only around seven minutes in order to give the horses a rest, the game was intense, a real workout, and Max felt drained after only six sets. *Definitely time for a beer.*

"Cheers!" The earl raised his glass as they sat on the polo-club patio. "Right, so as I was saying . . ."

The earl proceeded to continue a discussion they'd been trying to have while playing polo. A discussion about Sarah's behavior and how best to deal with it.

"It's not in her best interests to continue cavorting with someone beneath her class," Lord Pennington stated vehemently. "If Sarah is going to turn out well, she must be kept away from the likes of this Nick. And I want you to keep an eye on her, Max."

"Dad!" Max shook his head. His father had such a bee in his bonnet about class, and it bothered Max every time the earl mentioned it so blatantly. Not only did it seem unfair to judge a person based on what class they were born into, but it embarrassed Max to think that his father still operated in such an overtly snobbish way. And Max had heard enough for one morning, had kept his lip zipped during his father's tirades. But enough was enough. "Really, Dad, you don't know anything about Sarah's boyfriend," Max retorted defensively. "The fact that he isn't a nobleman doesn't make him a sleazebag by default."

The earl sighed, took another sip of his beer, wiped his hand across his mouth, and eyed Max with his shrewd, light blue eyes. "Max, I'm looking at the facts of the situation, and judging from what Headmistress Hern told me, this boy is bad news. Broken home, unemployed father, patchy academic record, and there is the small fact that he

80

happened to have ended up in your sister's bed! It's an old story. The lower classes simply do not mix well with the upper classes, like it or not. It's just a matter of breeding."

Max opened his mouth to respond, but his father was on a roll now and was rapidly listing the dangers of Sarah associating with those who "don't know better."

"She needs to be disciplined," the earl continued firmly. "Sarah is not from a common, vulgar background, and if I have to keep her under lock and key, I will ensure she learns her place in society!"

That'll help! Max thought sarcastically. Listening to his father, Max could only feel sorry for his sister. The man had a few good points, but he was also seriously out of touch, so obsessed with Sarah's status in society that he was unable to see Sarah as a person. As a teenage girl.

Gloomily Max stared out into the paddocks, watching as a resisting horse tried to pull away from its bit. *An apt metaphor,* he thought, feeling suddenly rather depressed. "If you rein Sarah in," Max argued, his eyes on the horse, "you'll only make her want to break out even more. And she'll hate you for it."

"That's just too bad," the earl hit back decisively. "I'd rather an alienated daughter than a pregnant one!"

Max frowned into his beer glass. He couldn't argue with his father on that point. After all, Sarah was teetering on the edge, and there were plenty of statistics to prove that their father had reason to worry. But despite the facts, Max knew that it wasn't a leash Sarah needed. She needed understanding, support, guidance. *She needs a mother,* Max thought, feeling defeated. Because for all the power and status their father had, and no matter how much he loved his daughter, there were some things he couldn't provide.

"And while we're on the subject of class, Max . . ." The earl frowned and folded his arms across his burly chest. "I'm not pleased with the familiarity I saw you exhibiting with the American kitchen maid at lunch."

Max felt his face redden slightly in surprise. He hadn't expected his father to bring this up. And it annoyed him in the extreme. His father had no business watching whom he spoke to and how. Plus Max was just chatting with Elizabeth. It was all perfectly harmless. For the most part . . .

"I'm not too old to catch on to the fact that you two were flirting," the earl continued. "And she's certainly a very nice and very pretty, poised girl. But you have your future to think of, Max. Specifically, your marriage to Lavinia, which is only going to strengthen your position in society."

"So you keep telling me, Father," Max replied dryly.

The earl sighed again and took a long pull on his beer. "My boy, I know you think I'm cold to bring up politics and marriage, but it's your interests I'm looking out for. Lavinia will make a lovely wife. And she will help propel you along on your career. You have duties and responsibilities. I just want to make sure you honor them."

Max felt a yawning hopelessness engulf him from the inside out as his father elaborated on what, exactly, family duty and honor meant. It wasn't that Max couldn't appreciate the earl's point of view. After all, his father had strong, admirable political ideals, took his position seriously, and always tried to use his influence to good end. He was philanthropic and fair. He didn't sit around wasting away like so many other idle aristocrats.

But Lord Pennington was also extremely old school, all about "the proper, right thing," all about not rocking the boat, putting family interests ahead of personal desire. Keeping the emotions inside so as to maintain a respectable outward appearance. Stiff upper lip and all that.

It made Max feel empty and hollow just hearing about it.

"A life in politics naturally means you shall have to do the expected thing," the earl lectured, his tanned face earnest and concerned. "Going against the grain isn't going to benefit you."

The expected thing: Lavinia. Against the grain: kitchen maids. The earl didn't have to spell it out for Max; he knew the implications. And he understood that doing the right thing by one's family did indeed count for something. But it also meant sacrifice, and Max hoped his father appreciated that.

"I was just being polite to Elizabeth," Max retorted stiffly, struggling to keep his anger in check. "Or has politeness gone out of fashion in political circles?"

But though Max's eyes flashed with indignation, and he had a good mind to say more, what was the use? He knew he wasn't about to convert the earl, so why waste his breath? His father was old school. You couldn't argue with the man.

Max pushed away his beer glass and stared moodily out into the paddocks, watching as their horses, Knight and Pollux, were brought back in for the next chukker. *I'm trapped,* Max thought, feeling a familiar sense of helplessness descend on him. Normally he tried not to think about the future, but it was coming, ready or not. And because of his title Max had little choice as to what, exactly, that future looked like.

In a way, he was doomed. Doomed to marry a

girl he was fond of but didn't really love and doomed to a life where his individuality always had to come last. *The price of privilege*, he reflected bitterly. *How lucky I am!*

"No, no time," the earl shouted to the groom who had signaled the horses were ready for more, cooled off and raring to go. The earl glanced at his Rolex and jumped to his feet. "Got to get back to Parliament for a late meeting," he explained to Max, straightening his V-necked navy sweater. "Guess they'll have to accept me looking like all hell," he added lightly, but Max was too lost in thought to respond.

"You go ahead and get back in the game. I'll have Mary send another chauffeur over," the earl concluded as he waved at Fenwick, his personal chauffeur. "And Max, please think about what I said. Watch your sister. And watch yourself."

With those parting words, the earl departed, leaving Max to contemplate the dregs of his beer and his life.

Neither of which looked too appetizing.

The coast is clear. Sarah smiled as she checked her watch, looked out of her bedroom window, and reconfirmed that her father's Rolls-Royce wasn't on the property. She knew it wouldn't be, but double checking didn't hurt, and Sarah was rewarded with an empty space where the car had been parked during lunch. *Fabulous!* With her father safely sandwiched between polo and Parliament, Sarah was free to slip off to school and keep her date with Nick.

Unless Mary catches me. The unpleasant thought wafted into Sarah's mind as she stalked over to her dressing table and began applying her makeup. Thinking of Mary made Sarah blanch beneath her translucent pearl blush. Things could get ugly if Mary was keeping her eyes peeled, and no doubt the pest would grill Sarah with questions if she saw her heading out. *And then log an entry into her spy journal!*

Sarah frowned, then suddenly the frown melted into a smile as she thought of Mary sniffing around. *Let her!* she thought, regarding her own reflection gazing back at her, looking unruffled. Mary could put out her feelers and act as nosy as all get out, but Sarah had a perfectly good excuse for needing to get back to school. After all, how could she do her homework without her schoolbooks? *Which I didn't exactly have a chance to pack when I was yanked out of there at 7 A.M.!*

Take that *to Daddy!* Sarah felt smug as she applied a second coat of Berry Beautiful lipstick by Chanteuse, her favorite Parisian makeup line. Then she mashed her lips together, did a final mascara check to see that she hadn't overdone it, grabbed her new Marks & Spencer pale green wool pea coat, and dashed out of her room.

Like clockwork! Sarah congratulated herself on a mission whose first task had been remarkably easy. It was a piece of cake to slip down the stairs and out the door unnoticed. The house felt so quiet, it was practically ringing with silence. Clearly Mary was busy lecturing the hired help, or maybe for once the woman was actually taking a break and attempting to lead a life of her own. *Not possible!* Sarah dismissed the idea as she made her way to the car park. Mary lived for Pennington House and for pleasing the earl.

She's not the only one, Sarah noted with irritation as she approached a line of parked cars. As expected, Percy, the youngest, most enthusiastic chauffeur, was lovingly attending to the earl's fleet, whistling as he rubbed a chamois leather cloth over the shiny black hood of a Mercedes.

"Percy, I need you to take me to school now," Sarah said extra loudly so as to interrupt his reverie.

Percy looked up, smiled at Sarah, and doffed his cap. "Yes, milady!" he replied. "I'd be happy to oblige you. Just allow me a moment to wipe the polish off your father's new Mercedes and I'll be with you presently."

Nervously Sarah glanced over her shoulder, suddenly convinced that Mary was peering out at her from a window. She snapped her head back toward Percy, who had begun his tremendously irritating trilling whistle again. "Percy, exactly which part of 'now' don't you understand?" Sarah hissed, her hands on her hips. She shook her head. *What a toss!* This was typical of Percy. The guy was so finicky and fussy about the cars, anyone would think he was an old man. *When in fact he could hardly be more than thirty!*

Sarah rolled her eyes and tapped her foot impatiently as Percy packed his things away with agonizing slowness. Did it look like she had all day? Sarah glowered at Percy until he opened the car door and let her in.

Finally! Sarah felt safer in the car than out, and her heart skipped lightly as the engine roared, then fell to a low, powerful purr. In only minutes she would be with Nick. Sarah closed her eyes and took a deep, satisfied breath. The day had gone so terribly slowly, and Sarah had spent most of the afternoon consoling herself after her spat with her father. But by trying on several different outfits and checking the time, she'd managed to lift her spirits a little.

And now here she was, in a simple dark gray A-line Calvin Klein dress with sling-back Swedish mules and just the right amount of lipstick. *If only Percy would get a move on instead of idling that engine!* Sarah glared fiercely at Percy and was about to open her mouth and yell when the car began to move.

Thank the pope! Sarah felt her stomach jolt in anticipation of her rendezvous with Nick, but at the same time she slunk down into her seat. Lying low wouldn't hurt as they passed through the grounds. Because though Sarah had excuses on hand for Mary, it would be so much simpler if she didn't have to use them at all . . .

Chapter Six

Nothing to report today. As usual. This task is proving more and more difficult with each day, and I'm beginning to feel desperate.

Vanessa put down her pen, folding her journal facedown on her rib cage, and lay back on her pillow, her gaze drifting up toward the ceiling. Yet another worthless day. Another day with nothing to show for itself.

In the background Alice cooed over Elizabeth's hair and eyes. "Your eyes are so blue. No—so aqua!!" she squeaked. Vanessa turned her face to the wall, trying to get as far away from the noise of her roommates as possible. *I've got to get out of here!* she thought miserably, suddenly violently seized with a desire to snatch her things together and leave on the next train. Sitting up, Vanessa began scribbling furiously into her journal, cataloging all the things she would do when she left Pennington and listing all the many things she would not miss about the place.

Such as the daily frustration she felt, which grew steadily with each hour that she continued to live in that hell pit without finding proof of her mother's involvement with the earl.

Nothing in the earl's suite today, Vanessa wrote in jerky, emphatic loops. *And not a thing last night either!*

Vanessa bit the end of her plastic Bic pen to keep from hurling it at the wall. She'd spent half of the previous night in the countess's suite again, scratching through mountains of clothes, boxes of photographs, her arms up to the elbows in cobwebs. But nothing even remotely promising had surfaced, and all Vanessa had to show for her troubles was an exhausted body and a steadily shriveling sense of purpose.

But maybe you were just too tired from the night before, Vanessa rationalized, realizing that if she continued to go down the hopeless track, then she truly would end up quitting. It was true, she could easily have missed something in the countess's suite. After all, the night before that, she'd spent several hours rifling through old boxes of junk in the storeroom, and exhaustion could easily have caused her to overlook something.

Still, though Vanessa knew she'd run out of steam and needed a good sleep before she'd get anywhere, her fingers itched to pick through more of the Penningtons' personal possessions. Unfortunately this afternoon's break had to be wasted, though, as there was an electrician in the earl's suite, attending to some faulty wiring.

Stuck here instead! Vanessa moped, feeling stranded on her bed, forced to suffer through Alice and Elizabeth when instead she could have had her hands on the proof by now. *If it even exists,* Vanessa amended darkly.

Don't give up hope! Vanessa commanded herself, then forced herself to write those words into her journal before she would lock it with the tiny gold key that hung from a chain around her neck, ensuring her secret wouldn't be read by prying eyes. But the words sounded empty and false and stupid to her. Sighing, Vanessa pushed the journal away, not yet ready to lock it away nor able to formulate any more fake words of optimism to put into it.

Maybe she *should* give up. She had no proof that any incriminating evidence still existed. The earl's affair was so long ago. Maybe it had all been buried under the carpet, never to be dragged out again.

And maybe this beneath-you job is all for nothing,

with no reward at the end, nothing except torture!
Vanessa continued on her downward spiral, her face hardening as she tried to ignore Alice's insufferable chirpiness in the background. Indeed, the job was torture, with its godforsaken chores and mindless minions like Alice. Vanessa knew that was mean, but she was feeling angry and resentful, two bloodred spots appearing in her cheeks as she considered the possibility that she had just wasted six months of her life, holding out for something that quite possibly didn't even exist.

You could be somewhere else, leading your own life instead of obsessing over your mother's! That part was undeniably true. Vanessa felt a spark of pain jolt through her insides as she thought of all the things she could be doing with herself. She was ambitious. She was eighteen and could be doing anything she wanted. She could be at university with the world at her fingertips. She could be studying fashion or film. Or working at a magazine or a TV station.

Vanessa's eyes took on a faraway glint as she pictured herself producing humorous pieces for a TV station, short, pithy style pieces or maybe even straight-up documentary news. . . .

The world is your oyster. The words floated up into her mind out of nowhere, and Vanessa knew they were true. She knew she had the smarts for a

TV job. Of course she'd have to prove herself and work her way up from the bottom, but that was no problem. *What could be worse than this?*

Even so, as Vanessa ran through the gazillion reasons she should leave Pennington House and compared them with the one reason she had for staying, she knew that no matter how awful and insufferable and thankless her job at Pennington was, she had to stay, and she had to give everything to her quest.

Because Vanessa knew she couldn't leave. She wasn't ready to take her place in the world. Not until she knew who she really was.

And could prove it beyond the shadow of a doubt.

This boy knows who I am. The real me. Sarah swooned as Nick crushed her with yet another of his demanding kisses, his mouth urgent and soft at the same time. Sarah had never been kissed the way Nick kissed her. And as his lips brushed searchingly against her own, Sarah felt like the kiss had gone right through her, rippling through her insides.

"You are so beautiful," Nick murmured softly, his hand cupping Sarah's chin gently.

So are you, she wanted to say, but of course she never would. Saying things like that to a boy wouldn't be right. Yet as Sarah looked into Nick's warm, brown eyes, fringed with long lashes, and the dark stubble on his tanned, cleft chin, she somehow felt that it wouldn't matter what she said to Nick. Anything she said, he would understand. That's how it felt between them. Natural. Honest. *And dangerous.*

Sarah anxiously looked up from Nick's kiss and peeped through a tangle of thorns in the rosebushes. Luckily the bushes were thick, so Percy wouldn't see her if he looked the wrong way. However, though they were hidden from Percy and students coming out of the Welles School, Sarah still felt a charge of nervousness, a tremor of danger. What they were doing was so forbidden. Her father had officially told her that if she disobeyed his orders, he would pull her out of school, and then she'd never even get to see Nick again, let alone kiss him!

But alarming as that thought was, Sarah also couldn't help feeling a slight, tingling thrill that she was doing something so totally risky and bold. She was here, with Nick, lying in the grass behind the rosebushes, kissing.

Breaking all the rules.

"You're my girl—you got that?" Nick tilted Sarah's chin and fixed her with an urgent, possessive, yet playful look. "Read me?"

"I read you," Sarah breathed, snuggling into Nick's chest.

"Don't you forget it," Nick mumbled, lightly stroking Sarah's hair. She couldn't help smiling. That was Nick. No frills, no fuss. Just calling it like it was and making his wishes known in the thick, slightly lilting East End accent that sent little shivers dancing all the way through Sarah's insides, goose bumping her shoulders. Nick had such a gruff, deep, sexy voice, and everything he said made her feel alive, safe, *real*.

He doesn't treat me like Lady Sarah Pennington, she mused happily, closing her eyes and breathing in Nick's strong, masculine scent mixed with the starch of his school shirt collar. *He treats me like a person. Like a woman . . .*

Nobody had ever treated Sarah the way Nick did. Everyone else acted like she was made of glass, but not Nick. He didn't ask her if he could kiss her; he just kissed her. And he didn't tone down his language or keep his negative thoughts to himself; he just said what was on his mind and didn't hide anything from her. *That's all I want.* Sarah traced the outline of Nick's broad back with her fingertips. *Someone to talk to. For real.*

This wasn't the first time Sarah had considered how special and unusual her connection to Nick was. It was odd, but ever since she'd met Nick, they'd seemed to just get each other. From the moment they'd locked eyes, it was like they were reading each other. She supposed it was chemistry, and she knew she had never felt anything like it before. With Nick, she actually felt like herself. Or at least she felt she could be herself and he would still care for her.

Sarah also felt that with Nick, she could be the opposite of herself—or at least the self she showed to the outside world. When she was with Nick, she could be vulnerable. Tender. Open. All the things she'd dreamed of being but had never been able to express. Instead she felt like she spent most of her life these days being angry and acting rudely, putting up walls around herself.

In some ways it seemed essential that she had to be that way if only to shut out the world she lived in. A world where everyone acted polite and poised even if they were feeling like hell.

But not here . . . Sarah leaned forward and placed a line of tiny kisses all the way from Nick's collarbone to his jaw, feeling woozy and wonderful and free.

That was another thing Nick had given Sarah. A passion she'd never even thought she was capable of, and she was constantly amazed by the strength of her feelings when Nick was holding her, her heart pounding like a gong.

"Sarah, I swear, I'd go insane if I couldn't see you," Nick muttered vehemently, grabbing a handful of Sarah's hair and bringing his lips to her neck.

Wow . . . Sarah's eyelids fluttered. She knew she'd never get used to the dizzying effect Nick had on her body, and it still thrilled her, the way his broad, strong hands seemed to know the shape of her. The strength of his biceps and the feel of his breath on her skin. It was like someone had wired her to an electrical outlet, and Sarah wasn't sure if she would melt or explode from the force of Nick's touch.

And best of all, she knew that Nick felt it too. They were totally in tune with each other on everything, and Sarah could feel that her pale skin and small frame had the same effect on Nick that his smooth, olive-tanned skin and big, lean body had on her. They were in so many ways opposites. *But opposites attract* . . .

"Don't worry, I won't let my dad get between us," Sarah said emphatically, sitting up and brushing a twig from her hair. "He can't stop me from caring about you, Nick, no matter how much power he has—or thinks he has. I won't—," she continued, sputtering with anger, but Nick sealed her lips with a soft, knowing kiss.

I'm so lucky. . . . Sarah tightened her arms

around Nick's back and let her cheek rest on the place where she could feel his heart beating. She could feel her own heart too, and the two seemed to be beating in time. Sarah knew it was corny to notice these things, but she couldn't help but marvel over the way she and Nick were so in sync. Right then, her cheek to his chest, she felt a surge, an actual wave of something vibrating through her. Something like . . . *love.*

The thought mesmerized her, as it did every time she thought it. And looking up at Nick's face, she could see that same feeling of love burning from him to her.

"I'm crazy about you, Sarah. I've never felt this way about anyone before," Nick burst out in typical Nick fashion, unable to keep anything to himself.

"Me neither," Sarah whispered, half wondering if all this were some sort of cruelly wonderful dream and she was about to wake up at Pennington House, sole alone except for snoopy servants and a father who didn't trust her.

But the force of Nick's hands gripping her own were nothing if not real. He squeezed her small palms tighter and fixed his big, dark eyes on Sarah's. "Let me prove it to you," he muttered hoarsely. "Let me make love to you."

Make love? Sarah's eyes widened, her heart feeling like it was either going to conk out or jump out of her chest and tear off down the school driveway. *Nick wants to make love to me!*

The idea was still sinking in, and even as Nick's questioning eyes searched her face, Sarah couldn't do much more than open her mouth. Her mind was spinning. *Sex.* Of course she'd thought about it a million times but never done it. Or even come close.

And now Nick, the most wonderful guy in the world, the hottest, most sensitive, most desirable boy in the school was telling her—Sarah—that he actually wanted to sleep with *her*.

She couldn't believe it.

Taking a deep breath, Sarah closed then opened her mouth again to answer Nick, her eyes suddenly, automatically flicking to the gap in the bushes from where she could see the glinting black door of her father's Mercedes. An image of her stern, forbidding, controlling father came to her then, and she bit her lip, suddenly afraid.

But just as quickly as it had arrived, Sarah forced the image of her father out of her mind. It had no right to be there. This was her life, her relationship, her moment. . . . *My brain!*

Sarah shifted her eyes from the hole in the bushes and refocused on Nick, on the two of them. She smiled. It was just a silly patch of lawn, but suddenly it seemed to Sarah as if they were on a magic carpet or in their own world. . . .

"I want you, Sarah," Nick repeated forcefully, and Sarah's pulse accelerated as she drank in his words.

"Nick—," she began, trembling as she formed the words she needed to answer him. "I need—"

But Nick didn't let Sarah finish and instead pulled her down on top of him to the grass until all she could see were his skin and hair and all she could feel was another suffocating, crushing, amazing, incredible kiss.

"Do you keep a journal?" Elizabeth queried. As Vanessa looked up from her writing, Elizabeth could tell she'd made a mistake by asking. *Maybe I intruded on her privacy,* she thought, biting her lip.

Or maybe I made the mistake of breathing! Elizabeth's inner voice chimed in.

That was probably it. And suddenly Elizabeth had had enough of Vanessa, enough of the black looks she kept shooting the world—like now—and Elizabeth vowed then and there to stop seeming so hesitant and eager to please around her. If Vanessa didn't want to be friends, then fine. Elizabeth was no longer prepared to go out of her way to be pleasant.

"Yes, I keep a journal," Vanessa responded sullenly. "And I also *lock* my journal so that people don't feel tempted to read what I think about them," she added, pursing her lips together into something faintly resembling a sardonic smile.

"Oh, I wouldn't worry about that," Elizabeth replied smoothly as she unpacked her toiletry bag. "I'm sure no one needs to read your journal to gauge your opinions."

Vanessa was silent for a moment, and Elizabeth felt a stab of self-righteous pleasure in having for once silenced the quick-witted, acid-tongued Vanessa. And then Vanessa laughed. Not a mean laugh, more like a small grunt of affirmation.

"Touché," Vanessa admitted rather grudgingly. Still, Elizabeth was pleased to see that Vanessa could take what she dished out.

"I keep a journal too," Elizabeth said, moving over to sit on her own bed, eager to break into more of a conversation and less of a sparring with words. "I've been doing it for years. I want to be a writer someday. Or a journalist. I haven't decided yet." As Elizabeth talked, she dipped into a tub of aloe-and-cucumber hand cream, which Alice had loaned her before leaving the room to attend to some chores for Mary.

Elizabeth couldn't believe how good the soothing, rich hand cream felt on her hands. And she also couldn't believe the state her hands were in after just one day of work. Rough, chapped, the skin red and chafed. Housework *was* hard. *You'll get used to it,* she told herself, wincing as she touched a small cut on her knuckle.

"You've never cleaned before, have you?" Vanessa asked. Elizabeth stiffened, waiting for an insult, but then she realized that Vanessa wasn't trying to rag on her. She was genuinely just asking.

"No. Just my room!" Elizabeth replied, her dimple flashing as she smiled, picturing her bedroom back at SVU, the way her room had always looked so neat, whereas Jessica's—

Before she could even finish the thought, Elizabeth was struck by a wave of intense pain and regret. It was still hard to believe that she and Jessica were estranged when they'd been joined at the hip their whole lives.

But she had to put it out of her mind. What Jessica had done was irreversible. *No use in dwelling on the past!*

"You're homesick," Vanessa stated, narrowing her eyes and regarding Elizabeth shrewdly. "There's somebody you really miss. I can tell."

And there's nothing you don't *miss!* Elizabeth was part alarmed and part impressed by Vanessa's quickness—alarmed because she didn't want to give too much away.

"Well, of course I have family and friends who I left behind," she answered elusively, spreading

104

lotion into the creases of her elbows. She had to be careful what she said to Vanessa. Not that Vanessa would care what her story was; Elizabeth knew that. *But since you started this Elizabeth Bennet secrecy thing, you'd better stick with it!*

"Uh, tell me again when Max's wedding is?" Elizabeth abruptly changed the subject and turned her face from Vanessa's prying eyes. It wasn't just her background she didn't want Vanessa digging into; Elizabeth also didn't want Vanessa to suspect any hint of interest in Max, so she kept her face impassive and her eyes on her hands, hoping instead that Vanessa might simply interpret the question as an innocent one. Which it was. Pretty much.

"Six long, agonizing months." Vanessa sighed. Then suddenly, suspiciously, she added sharply, "What's it to you?"

"My job?" Elizabeth retorted easily, but she knew Vanessa wasn't fooled and . . . *so what?* So Elizabeth thought Max was cute. It wasn't a crime. Thinking wasn't doing, and if she couldn't share her thoughts with her own roommate, then who would she be able to share them with?

Get real! Elizabeth slapped a dollop of lotion onto her elbow and grimaced. Though she would have loved to be able to have a little girl talk with Vanessa, she knew she was kidding herself. Vanessa might have been vaguely more tolerant of her during this conversation, but Elizabeth doubted they were about to become bosom buddies.

"You're interested in Max, aren't you?" Vanessa grilled her, and Elizabeth felt her face flush a telltale bloodred. Apparently it was too late to hide her thoughts. Vanessa had already sniffed them out.

"Learn your colors," Vanessa quipped, and Elizabeth looked up, confused. "Blue blood and red blood don't mix!"

Elizabeth smeared lotion in silence as Vanessa launched into a scathing lecture about royals and commoners, Max and Elizabeth.

"The sooner you stop *fantasizing,* the easier your *reality* will be," Vanessa stated vehemently, thumping her journal in her palm for emphasis. "Max would only use and abuse you, Elizabeth. It's the royal way," she continued, running a hand impatiently through her cap of gleaming black hair. "And believe me, if you mess around with Max, the duchess Lavinia will have you for breakfast. You *don't* want to cross her."

Of course, Vanessa was right, but Elizabeth couldn't quite hide the disappointment that welled up inside her and expelled itself in the form of a sigh. Vanessa made perfect sense, but it all still seemed rather ridiculous and unfair to Elizabeth.

No one ought to have the right to decide who liked whom. Plus Max didn't seem to be nearly as awful as Vanessa claimed he was. *Use and abuse . . .* would he really treat anyone that way? Elizabeth instinctively doubted it, just as instinctively she doubted Max was in love with his fiancée.

But as soon as that thought entered her head, Elizabeth chastised herself for even going there. How did she know what was in Max's heart? She'd barely even spoken to him!

Yet though Elizabeth rationalized the obvious points to herself with each emphatic kneading of her arms and elbows, she still couldn't quite rid herself of her instinctive impressions of Max. He was the one person she felt connected to in this house. She'd never be able to explain it to anyone, but she'd felt something pass between them, a mutual affinity, some kind of wordless understanding. . . .

Or maybe it's just your imagination! Decisively Elizabeth replaced the lid on the pot of lotion and lifted her chin, determined to regroup, to get her act together. Vanessa had a point, and no amount of wishful thinking could change it: *If I don't accept my place, I'll get hurt . . . or worse, fired!*

In the middle of that gloomy thought Alice returned from her chores and disrupted the somber scene by suggesting a night on the town. "There's a hot new club I'd like to try," she babbled happily, clearly oblivious to the mood. "We could dress up," she urged Elizabeth. "Maybe I could borrow some of your clothes . . . and get some makeup tips," she added shyly, training her hopeful brown eyes on Elizabeth. "I like the way you do your makeup. You're very pretty, you are."

Poor Alice. Elizabeth couldn't help feeling sorry for the eighteen-year-old. She was sweet, but Vanessa was right: She was somewhat clueless and also didn't have much confidence. In many ways she seemed younger than she was.

"So what do you say, girls?"

"No can do, Alice." Vanessa refused Alice's suggestion swiftly, turning back to her journal. "I've already got plans," she added mysteriously.

"How about it, Liza?" Elizabeth smiled at the nickname Alice had given her. It was so old-fashioned. Kind of like Alice, who in all ways reminded Elizabeth of the typical plain-Jane servant girl of PBS period-piece productions.

"Sorry, Alice, I'm just so wiped today," Elizabeth apologized, wincing as Alice's face fell. *I'll make it up to her,* Elizabeth promised herself, knowing that Alice could benefit from some fun. She'd been having a rough time with Mary lately, and Elizabeth had spotted her sniffling earlier in the scullery.

But unfortunately Elizabeth just didn't have an ounce of energy left after her first day on the job. She'd worked extra hard trying to learn the ropes, and all she wanted was a bubble bath and bed. She was still suffering from jet lag too. "Another time," she added, annoyed to spot Vanessa rolling her eyes. *Obviously she thinks I'm a total dullard,* Elizabeth reflected. *So much for our bonding session! So much for my thinking that—*

But Elizabeth was interrupted midthought by a sharp rap on the door, followed by an image of Mary Dale, who bustled in purposefully, her face drawn and her eyes shining angrily. *Uh-oh!*

"Which one of you left a dirty pail of soap water by the back door?" Mary demanded, her voice cold and clipped. "A pail I almost tripped over?"

Elizabeth scrambled to look less relaxed on her bed, her heart thumping with the force of Mary's shrill, angry voice.

"Do I look as if I have all night? Do you think I ask questions for my *health*? Or is someone planning on gracing me with an answer!" Mary ranted, her hands on her ample hips. She was so livid with anger that she was shaking, but no one said a word. Mary's outburst was met with a silence so still, you could hear a pin drop.

"If I don't get an answer right now, you will all

be docked an hour's pay!" Mary continued, glaring at each of them. "Whoever did it, I'm giving you one more chance to speak up, or else you'll be taking the others down with you!"

Could it have been me? Elizabeth racked her brains, wondering for a fleeting second if she could have forgotten to hurl out a pail of dirty water.

But one look at Alice's frightened, guilty face and Elizabeth knew for sure it hadn't been her own mistake. Or Vanessa's. Alice's face was a dead giveaway, and she squirmed in the doorway, looking like at any moment she would dissolve into tears—or at least into a confession.

This is trouble! Elizabeth thought as the silence grew into a yawning gap. And in that silence Elizabeth's heart went out to Alice. From the look on Mary's face, Elizabeth knew there would be no second chances for Alice.

The girl was toast.

"Gosh, Nick, I . . . don't know what to say!" Sarah murmured when they finally broke their kiss for air. It was true. She didn't know what to say to Nick's suggestion. The idea was still swimming through her brain, and she didn't have the first clue what to think, much less what to say to him. Plus the force field of electricity crackling around her as she tried to recover from yet another round of heady, delicious kisses only made Sarah feel woozier and less capable of clear thinking.

"Say yes," Nick murmured into her ear, his hands roving across her back. "Say you want to."

But I don't know I do! Sarah was dying to blurt out the words, to say something, at least, but she wasn't sure she even could. *Sex!* The word itself produced all these conflicting emotions in Sarah, from fear to excitement and back to fear. Especially fear.

"Oh, I don't know if I can give you an answer . . . yet," Sarah finally replied with a coy, mysterious smile, even though her heart was slamming full force into her rib cage. "Maybe we can chat about this later?" she suggested smoothly, leaning in for another kiss and hoping to distract Nick until she at least had some time to think everything over by herself.

"When?" Nick pulled away from Sarah, his face stricken and passionate. "Your father's keeping you away from me, and I can't even be with you alone. Your chauffeur's in the car right this very minute!" he burst out impatiently, squeezing Sarah's arms.

Nick was right. Of course. From now on they'd have to steal moments together. They'd be lucky if they even got a private moment once a week, let alone every day. It was murder. But that still didn't help Sarah with her decision. It only made her feel more panicked, more pressured by time and circumstance.

"I'm not sure the timing is right," Sarah said finally, feeling a cold, gnawing pinch at her insides as she watched Nick's face fall in disappointment. Then she felt a swell of love for him as he struggled to hide his disappointment so as not to make her feel bad.

"I mean . . . I'm just not sure about . . . anything." Sarah trailed off weakly. She knew she was being less than eloquent, but she couldn't help it. She was tongue-tied because she was confused. Was timing the problem, or was it that she was simply scared? And was being scared natural, or was it a sign she wasn't ready? *And how will I know when I'm ready?* Sarah wondered anxiously. *Does anyone ever really know?*

"You don't need to be sure of everything," Nick said finally, in a sweet, low voice. "Just be sure about us." His hand gently traced Sarah's cheek, and she closed her eyes, his words soothing the babble in her head. "We're a pair! " Nick continued as he pulled Sarah to his chest and crushed her. "We're like . . . soul mates. I honestly don't know what I'd do if you weren't in my world," he spoke into her hair.

Soul mates. Sarah felt a burst of warmth spreading through the base of her neck and up through the roots of her hair. Hearing Nick say it made her realize, once again, that he truly did care for her.

"It sounds revoltingly mushy, but I really do believe it," Nick added, stroking Sarah's head. "You may be Lady P. and I'm just some poor sod from the East End, but we're on the same page."

Sarah leaned into Nick's shoulder, a smile on her lips as he went into a litany of all the things they had in common, from food to music to TV to both hating circuses! *Nicholas Jones,* she thought lovingly. *How could I ever regret sleeping with you?*

Being with Nick felt so familiar and safe and exciting all at once. And Sarah knew instinctively that sleeping with him would just feel right too. When it happened.

But she wasn't sure it should happen yet.

"You know I'm a virgin," Sarah said suddenly, shyly, blushing at the thought.

"And you know I'd be very gentle," Nick replied, staring deeply into her eyes. "You also know how much I adore you, Sarah. You do, right?"

"Yes . . . I know." Sarah did know. She didn't have any doubts about that.

"You know that you mean the world to me,

113

and I'd rather die, I swear, than ever hurt you," Nick continued, gripping Sarah's arms. "But this won't hurt us. It'll make us a real couple. Totally together, know what I mean?"

Sarah thought she knew. No, she *did* know what Nick meant, and it did give her a jolt to think of them as one, as a real couple, sealing their relationship. Making love.

And she should be ready for it. She believed and trusted Nick; she knew he was sincere; she was sixteen years old. *What more do you need?* Sarah asked herself. Plus if sex was so scary and terrifying, then no one would ever do it. And half of Sarah's friends had done it. Or at least they said they had . . .

And what if she didn't do it? Sarah stared back into Nick's dark, intense, soulful eyes. He was a good guy—a great guy—with a huge heart. But she also knew he was just a guy, and guys couldn't wait around forever. Not if there were other girls ready to do it. And Sarah knew there were at least five girls who would line up to steal Nick away from her if they had half a chance . . .

So then she should do it.

Or at least she should *consider* doing it.

"I think I'll say . . . maybe," Sarah said at last, a playful smile pulling at the corners of her mouth even as her eyes were serious. "Is maybe okay?"

"So long as I get to see you every day this week," Nick replied, gently kissing the tip of her nose. "Even if it's just at break time, I don't care."

At that moment Sarah felt assured that whatever she decided, she was at least deciding it with the right guy. Telling her he needed to see her every day. That was just the sort of thing that Nick said, the sort of thing that made Sarah feel incredibly special, but in a real, not a cheesy, way. Because Nick just plain *said* it, without sugaring his words or doing daft things like writing her poetry or anything else poncey and phony.

Writing poetry. Sending stiff, waxy flower arrangements. All those courtly gestures that Sarah had witnessed her cousins Julia and Eustacia going through. That sort of thing passed for romance in her family circles. *But not in my book.* Smiling, Sarah pictured her father's horrified face if he could see her idea of romance: roses picked off the bush by Nick and handed to her as they lay on the lawn instead of roses delivered via courier from some baron or other such nobleman. . . .

Oops! Suddenly Sarah shot to her feet as her thoughts looped back to Pennington House. And to the fact that her father had forbidden her to see Nick. And would be almost home by now!

Fearfully Sarah smoothed her dress and pulled a bramble from her hair. "I've got to run," she said hurriedly to Nick as he pulled her toward him for a last kiss.

"Just think about this: I want to make love to you this weekend. At my house," Nick whispered in her ear as she pulled away. "I would make it very special, I promise," he added, taking her face in his hands and planting a light kiss on her cheek before stepping back. "Consider it."

"Maybe," Sarah replied as Nick walked slowly backward, his hair tousled, his tie at an angle. He looked unbelievably sexy, and she felt desperately sad to watch him walk away, knowing she had to get in the damned car with Percy and head off home. As opposed to if she *hadn't* been pulled out of boarding school. If she were still a boarder, she could be lolling about on the lawns with Nick for at least another hour before the dinner bell.

It was only as Sarah waved Nick a last good-bye that she suddenly registered Nick's parting words properly: *I want to make love to you this weekend. At my house.*

Alarm zigzagged up through the base of her spine. *This weekend?* Suddenly Sarah felt like she had motion sickness even though her feet were planted firmly on terra firma.

Sex. In a matter of days. *Possibly too much.* Definitely *too soon!*

*   *   *

"I'll ask you one last time. Who forgot the dirty pail of water?" Mary tapped her foot impatiently on the floor.

You're enjoying this, aren't you? Vanessa couldn't exactly send Mary hateful glances, but she could shoot her hate vibes. The woman was practically frothing at the mouth—and all because of a stupid pail of dirty water. Big deal.

But Vanessa knew in Mary's world, this was a big deal. She liked to run a tight ship, and an oversight like this was just the sort of thing Mary kept her eye out for.

Which all meant big trouble for Alice.

An arrow of sympathy shot through Vanessa as she observed poor, miserable Alice. Her ashen face and tearing eyes made it dead obvious. As was the way she was twisting her hands together and sort of squirming into the wall as if she hoped it would open up and swallow her.

She knows what's coming, Vanessa reflected, pity clouding her eyes as she watched Alice blink and tremble. The none-too-bright Alice had been getting into a lot of trouble lately for her forgetfulness and general "slovenliness," as Mary put it. And Vanessa knew that an infraction like this, mild as it was, would most likely be the straw that broke the camel's back. *She'll be fired!*

Vanessa watched as Alice opened and closed

her mouth like a fish. But nothing came out. Clearly the girl was too terrified to confess.

"Well, girls, you give me no choice but to dock all of you an hour's pay!" Mary exclaimed, her eyes shining with anger as she glared at each one of them.

"That's not fair!" Vanessa shot back, staring Mary down. She wasn't afraid of her, and she wouldn't stand there and take Mary's wrath. *All of this for a bloody bucket of water?* It was ridiculous. And Vanessa wasn't afraid to say so.

"You can't punish everyone for one person's mistake," Vanessa continued coolly. "Especially since it was, after all, just a mistake . . ." *Oh, boy,* Vanessa thought, watching Mary's twitching face. She was about to reach boiling point. She wasn't used to being talked back to. But Vanessa knew she had to continue babbling because at least this way she was deflecting Mary's attention from Alice, who had guilt written all over her mousy, terror-stricken face.

And though Vanessa wasn't exactly thrilled with Alice for causing all three of them to lose their wages, she didn't think the idiot should lose her job either. Best to keep talking and keep Mary's anger directed at someone who could handle it.

"You shut your trap, Vanessa!" Mary burst out

angrily, wagging a finger at her. "You've been skating on very thin ice lately. If I were you, I'd watch my mouth!"

Oh, get lost, granny! Vanessa was dying to say this to Mary, who looked at that moment exactly like the Wicked Witch of the West in her severe black dress, her eyes as cold as ice and full of venom. All she needed was the broomstick. But Vanessa could only glare back at Mary and hope that she had finished her little tirade and would now leave their room.

"I did it," a trembling yet clear voice broke in. Elizabeth's voice. "I'm sorry," she added, her pale face peeping out from behind her curtain of blond hair. "I just forgot."

No, you didn't. Vanessa's eyes widened as she took in the image of Elizabeth trying to look guilty. Mary had instantly snapped her head around, and now Elizabeth stood there, solemnly accepting Mary's inflamed words with her head bowed in apology. An apology Vanessa knew full well Elizabeth wasn't responsible for giving.

"I must say I am surprised. That was very sloppy of you, and I did not expect you to be the culprit here, Elizabeth," Mary prattled on, but her tone, though angry, was easily calmer than when she'd been dealing with Vanessa. "I shall be docking you two hours' pay to teach you a lesson."

Elizabeth nodded weakly, and Mary, satisfied at last, prepared to leave the room. "I'm sorry I have to do it," she added bluntly, a flicker of what might pass for sympathy clouding her angry eyes. "It is your first day on the job and all. But that's no excuse. One must be attentive at all times."

"Yes, Mary," Elizabeth murmured dutifully, keeping her head lowered until Mary left the room.

"Oh, Elizabeth, I can't believe you just did that!" Alice sobbed, convulsing in tears of relief and shame. "I'm so, so, so sorry! And thank you, thank you, thank you!" she sniveled, hurling her arms around Elizabeth's waist. "You saved me. My job was on the line."

Vanessa said nothing, but her eyes held the question from across the room, and Elizabeth answered immediately. "I knew Mary would go easier on me," she explained. "I'm new. I haven't made any mistakes yet, so she can't very well fire me over this."

"I'll pay you back, I swear it, every penny!" Alice declared vociferously, still clinging to Elizabeth as Vanessa mulled over Elizabeth's words. It was true; Elizabeth was relatively safe from Mary compared to the others. And Alice especially. But still. She'd stuck out her neck for Alice, whom she barely even knew. And lost two hours of pay for her trouble!

"It's okay, Alice." Elizabeth patted her on the back and gently extracted herself from the girl's forceful embrace. "We've got to stick together, right?"

As Alice snuffled through more thanks and apologies, Vanessa remained silent, still thinking over Elizabeth's actions. By incurring Mary's wrath, Elizabeth had managed to tarnish the perfect first impression she'd made on the staff. And lost money in the process. And had to endure a public humiliation and lecture by Mary, which Vanessa considered to be far worse than losing any amount of money. *But she did it anyway. . . .*

Vanessa kept her mouth closed. The thought of praising Elizabeth the Martyr was a bit too much for her. She thought the words might get stuck in her throat.

Still, Vanessa couldn't help the spark of admiration and surprise that showed through in her eyes. It was cool of Elizabeth to have done what she did. It showed character and courage, two things Vanessa hadn't spotted in Elizabeth until now.

Vanessa turned back to her journal and began scribbling. *Elizabeth Bennet—or whoever she is,* Vanessa wrote, *is turning out to have some spunk.*

A day of surprises after all!

Chapter Seven

Another chapter of hell! Sarah stared grimly ahead of her as the Rolls-Royce coasted out of Pennington's iron gates on a chilly Wednesday morning. Beside her, her father rattled the morning paper and read in silence.

A silence that felt to Sarah like it was louder than a scream.

Sarah closed her hands into fists so tight, she could see the skin turn white over her knuckles. If only just for once she could turn to her father, open her mouth, and really yell! Sarah felt that if she could do it only once, it would help her feel like an actual person instead of a zombie.

But of course that was "simply not done." And Sarah knew that if she opened her mouth now, she would only get herself into deeper trouble than she was already.

So instead she focused on glaring at Fenwick, her father's chauffeur, training her fiery gaze into his rearview mirror, her skin prickling under her school blazer, her hair itching under the stupid straw basher that all Welles students had to wear.

Rat! Sarah messaged angrily as her gaze bore into the rearview mirror, meeting Fenwick's small, expressionless blue eyes. Percy had told Fenwick about Sarah's escapade the day before. Or at least what he knew of it. Which was that Sarah had asked him to take her to school and had spent hours there. And naturally, tattletale that he was, Fenwick had run it by his lord and master.

Which meant an earful at breakfast for Sarah.

Anger blazed red-hot up through the soles of her feet as Sarah recounted the awful blasting she'd received at breakfast. Her father hadn't been able to prove it, but he'd accused her of being "up to something" no matter how many times she'd told him she was simply fetching her schoolbooks and finding out about the classes she'd missed.

But of course her father didn't believe her. *He never trusts me!* Sarah thought gloomily, her eyes flickering briefly to the right, meeting a wall of newsprint.

Of course, there *was* the small matter that Sarah was lying. *But that's beside the point!* Sarah thought huffily, crossing her arms. Her father wouldn't believe her even if she *were* telling the truth. Even if she hadn't met up with Nick behind the rosebushes.

Thinking of Nick and their dizzying embraces on the school lawn, Sarah felt suddenly light-headed and tremulous, remembering his proposal. She'd barely even been able to sleep the night before, she'd been so caught up in The Decision. And she still hadn't got past maybe. *Which isn't exactly a decision,* she reminded herself as the Rolls-Royce rounded a corner onto a small highway lined with stone walls.

"You know, your Nick can't be such a terrific chap if he'd risk getting you into trouble by actually getting into your *bed*. Have you thought of that?" The earl spoke up suddenly from behind his newspaper, and an icy shock quivered through Sarah. How did her father know she was thinking of Nick?

But after a moment Sarah realized the odds were probably ten to one that at any given point she'd be thinking of Nick. And her father was still smarting over what he insisted on calling—in his exaggerated, pompous way—Sarah's "breach of conduct!"

"He must be a good-for-nothing because he's encouraging you to act like one!" the earl continued, and Sarah narrowed her eyes, wishing she were old enough to drive herself to school, wondering why her father couldn't just follow her example and shut up. Hadn't he ranted enough for one morning?

But Sarah could tell he was only just warming up, and so she kept her eyes stiffly fixed ahead of her and concentrated instead on an image of Nick's face, his broad, rugby-muscled back and his big, strong hands. . . .

". . . You've been acting irresponsibly, so now you have to be restrained." The earl's words were more like background noise now. Like a radio DJ blathering on about some random happening that Sarah had no interest in. She had much more important things to think of. Or rather, one really massively important thing to ponder, with dire consequences looming all around it.

". . . And I'm warning you," the earl nattered on, but Sarah was doing an excellent job of blotting out the meaning of his speech, so that instead of English, the words were all smooshing together and beginning to sound instead like some other language. Some distantly related cousin of English. Gaelic or Welsh. Medieval Scottish.

But the words in her own head were very decidedly modern English. *Yes. Or no.*

A sliver of panic prickled at Sarah's insides. When Nick had first brought up the whole question of sex, she'd imagined it would be sometime in the near future if it happened at all. But she'd never pictured it would be this weekend! *Only days away.* And now, having an actual date set for the possible losing of her virginity made Sarah feel queasy.

And excited.

How can I feel all these things at once? She sighed, wishing again for the thousandth time that she had an older sister to talk to. Or her mother. Sarah knew that if her mother were still alive, they'd be close enough to talk about these kinds of things. Her mother would have advice, something clever to say. Something that would help Sarah figure out what was right for her.

But instead the closest thing she had to a sister was Lavinia. *Who wouldn't know love or any other strong feeling if it smacked her in the face!*

And the closest thing Sarah had to a mother was Mary. True, Mary had known Sarah all her life, but the thought of talking to Mary about sex . . . ! Sarah doubted Mary had even *had* sex before.

The thought was ridiculous and horrific and absurd and *embarrassing.* Especially so early in the morning! Sarah snorted with a mixture of disgust and amusement. At which point her father went suddenly silent, clearly thinking the snort was aimed at him.

Sarah turned to her father and opened her

mouth to try to explain, but he merely regarded her frostily and then disappeared behind his newspaper.

Good old-fashioned Pennington communication! Sarah bit her lip, repressing a sigh. There was no point in even trying to talk to her father. They were long past the stage where they could make sense of each other. Plus she knew her father wouldn't listen to her even if she tried to speak. He'd delivered his monologue and had gone back to shutting her out with his newspaper in her face.

The way he always did.

Sarah turned her head to look out the window. Fifteen minutes in the car and the landscape hadn't changed. Long, empty stretches of lonely field occasionally broken by copses of thin, straggling trees. And it all belonged to the Pennington estate.

Somehow this made her sad.

I don't even know where to begin, Elizabeth wrote. *The last few days have been somewhere between a dream and a nightmare. I guess only time will tell which. . . .*

She paused, put down her pen, and looked up. From where she sat, tucked away on a circle of grass near the Pennington rose garden, things couldn't have looked more idyllic. A scent of rose petals wafted by on a light breeze, and Elizabeth inhaled the delicate scent and smiled. The gardens truly were spectacular, and Elizabeth felt like she was floating on an oasis of green grass, having a moment of peace and quiet all to herself. Floating away from her duties, away from the mad scramble of the scullery, Mary's hot temper, and everything else that came along with life at Pennington House. Floating . . .

Stifling a yawn, Elizabeth forced herself to sit up. She'd almost drifted off even though it was only early afternoon and her break would soon be over. But she still felt the jet-lag combination of sleepiness and disorientation. It was either that or the effects of so much backbreaking work. . . .

I never, ever, in my wildest dreams, thought I'd end up working as a kitchen maid, Elizabeth scribbled. *But if life didn't surprise us, then we would never learn anything about ourselves. We'd stay forever cocooned in our small worlds, watching time turn us into little people, afraid of anything that didn't come preplanned, prepackaged, prearranged. . . .*

Elizabeth put down her pen and read. Her writing surprised her a little. It seemed slightly rambling and unfocused, but also loose and kind of interesting.

Since her last semester of classes Elizabeth had begun to pay attention to the rhythms of her sentences, on the advice of one of her writing instructors. And though she was just writing in her journal, Elizabeth always paid attention to the way her words came out on the page. After all, if she was going to be a writer someday . . .

"Are you a writer?"

Elizabeth looked up, startled by the voice. And the question, a question she had at that very moment been considering.

Max waved his pen at her, and Elizabeth smiled, her heart suddenly, almost imperceptibly, skipping a beat. When had he appeared on the stone wall that curved around the rose garden? How long had he been watching her?

"I, uh, yes, I . . . hope so." Elizabeth stumbled over a response, self-consciousness burning up through the back of her neck. Even though he couldn't read her words or her thoughts, Elizabeth felt suddenly strange at the idea of someone—especially Max—watching her in a private moment of self-reflection. It felt somehow . . . intimate.

And as Max swung his lean body over the wall and drifted over toward her, Elizabeth felt another tremor of nervousness, a reflexive anxiety. Was she on off-limits turf? *Is part of the garden for the family only?* She couldn't remember exactly. And she also knew she couldn't afford to get into trouble again, not after taking the fall for Alice—which had turned Mary a bit sour on Elizabeth.

But Max didn't seem to act like anything was awry, and so Elizabeth concluded that servants probably were allowed in that part of the garden.

"I've been doing the same thing you have," Max said as he approached Elizabeth, holding up a leather-bound notebook and a small silver pencil. "May I?" he added, gesturing at the square of grass next to her. Elizabeth nodded, annoyed at the way her heart seemed to lurch again as Max lowered himself to the grass, exposing a sliver of taut, muscled stomach as he lay down.

Nervously Elizabeth cleared her throat. Then she frowned, ordering herself to relax and stop acting skittish as if she were in the sixth grade and Max was the first guy she'd ever thought was cute. "So you're a writer too?" she ventured.

"I wish." Max smiled ruefully. "I'd like to write a novel, but I'm studying a PPE at Oxford—politics, philosophy, and economics," he explained. "It's the family tradition. Well, actually, it's what all noblemen's sons study," he added, his smile turning ironic. "A real bunch of originals, aren't we?"

"It doesn't sound so bad," Elizabeth replied, feeling herself loosen up as Max chattered on, describing his course work and his thesis. "You know, lots of writers have other careers. Some of the best ones, I think."

"What about you?" Max leaned on his elbow, studying Elizabeth with his warm, intelligent eyes. "How does a writer survive working in the Pennington kitchen? It must be insufferable!"

"No, it's not. It's experience. It's the real world," Elizabeth replied, trying to remain unruffled by the proximity of Max's long, ropy body and sexy, slightly pouty mouth. He really was unbelievably gorgeous, his classic features accentuated by his graceful physique and low, gentle voice. *I bet he's on the rowing team,* Elizabeth mused absently, her eyes drifting to linger on Max's broad shoulders.

Will you stop? she castigated herself immediately after, dragging her eyes away from Max's chest area, a flash of heat reddening her cheeks.

Embarrassed, Elizabeth looked down and picked a blade of grass. She felt she was being somehow totally, ridiculously obvious—which wasn't her style at all. Yet it seemed Max hadn't picked up on anything because when she stole another look, he appeared totally self-possessed and was still chatting about school and studying and writing, asking her questions about her own plans.

"So you were planning on studying journalism at the University of London?" he prompted.

"No, creative writing," Elizabeth explained, launching into a short history of her switch out of journalism and toward fiction. "I just find fiction much freer," she explained. "In fiction you can be anyone, tell any story you like. Invent everything. And get to make real life interesting even when it's boring," she continued, warming up. "Anything can come alive in fiction, and every experience suddenly seems useful."

Max's face lit up. "I know exactly what you mean."

And as they talked first about writing, then their favorite writers and the kinds of stories they liked, Elizabeth felt herself growing more and more relaxed. It was really easy to talk to Max. They had similar ideas on so many things. Weird coincidences that made them seem connected: Both loved Virginia Woolf, but neither of them had managed to finish Joyce's *Ulysses*. Both of them ranked E. M. Forster's *Howards End* among their top-ten favorite novels of all time as well as Faulkner's *The Sound and the Fury*.

Watching Max's animated expression as they talked about writing, Elizabeth couldn't help feeling amazed at the way they got on so well. She'd known she liked Max from the beginning, but it was weird to find out they had so much in common.

"Of course, writing is my secret passion," Max remarked wistfully after a short but comfortable silence following the tail end of their enthusiastic conversation.

"Why secret?" Elizabeth asked, resting her chin on her knees.

"My father expects me to follow him into Parliament, not write novels," Max explained with a dry laugh. "Once I'm done with my thesis, that's the end of my freedom."

Elizabeth considered this as their eyes drifted into the distance, where Davy was instructing gardeners on where to plant baby cypress trees and other small shrubs. *Poor Max.* She couldn't help feeling sorry for him. He had everything money could buy. *But money can't buy you freedom.*

At that, Elizabeth's thoughts turned to her own parents. Though they were hardly aristocrats following traditions, they had their own expectations and ultimatums and would hardly approve of what Elizabeth was doing now. In that way, she felt she could relate to Max.

I wonder what he's thinking now, Elizabeth mused, shifting her eyes to Max, who was enigmatically appraising the landscaping that was taking place around them. Landscaping for his upcoming wedding.

Maybe this is all evidence to Max of the trapped life he was born into, a life where everything is planned, laid out in advance. . . . Elizabeth thought about this, looking from Max to Davy and his men, who were busily maneuvering a small tree into a hole in the ground.

But in thinking about Max's perfectly laid out life, and watching the garden being shaped by Davy's men, Elizabeth realized that though she and Max both had parents who monitored their lives, she was free in a way that Max could never be. Here, now, at Pennington, away from her parents and her home, Elizabeth was living a totally unexpected life, a life that no one—least of all Elizabeth herself—could have foreseen.

"Do you miss your home?" Max asked at that moment, his question once again, Elizabeth noticed, strangely connecting to her thoughts.

But before she had time to answer, a stout figure suddenly bustled through the trees and came down from the path. "Max, Lavinia's on the phone," Mary said evenly, though her eyes flashed a sudden disapproval and surprise at seeing Elizabeth on the lawn next to Max.

"Oh . . ." An unreadable mix of emotions flickered across Max's face, and he turned slightly red as he scrambled to his feet. "Be right there."

As Elizabeth watched Max and Mary leave, she suddenly felt like a bit of an idiot. The phone call from Lavinia was a reality check, reminding Elizabeth of the fact that Max had a real, other life, a life she knew nothing about. *We may be similar as people,* Elizabeth realized, *but we operate in totally different worlds.* Those were the facts; the rest was just fiction.

So get over it! Elizabeth reprimanded herself, reopening her journal with purpose. *After all, you came out here to write, not flirt!*

Oh, God, give me strength! Sarah stifled a yawn as she stared gloomily at Lavinia. Sarah was so bored, she was practically in a coma. How had she agreed to this afternoon of skull-numbing dreariness, this bridal fitting, which felt more like a trip to the morgue than a joyous occasion? *How?* Sarah asked herself incredulously. *Oh, that's right: Max.* Max had asked Sarah to go on a gown consultation with Lavinia, and since he was her only ally, Sarah had agreed.

Oh, Max . . . Sarah genuinely feared for her brother as she stared at Lavinia's pinched face and heard her emit yet another whine, all in her trademark detached, whispery voice.

"Can we not find something more original?" Lavinia mewed as a couturier scuttled across the floor, carrying a roll of stunning, shimmering raw silk from Thailand, which Lavinia simply stared at, her perfect features contorting into a frown. "I mean, can we not find something less *boring?*" She sighed.

Good point! Sarah shook her head as she surveyed Lavinia. Perfect, china-doll face. Aristocratic high cheekbones, smooth porcelain skin, naturally red perfectly bowed lips, and sky blue eyes delicately fringed by thick, curling eyelashes. Her perfect head rested on a long, swan's neck, her mane of ice blond hair was pulled back into an expert, impossibly chic chignon. And then there was Lavinia's perfectly slim figure clad in a flesh-toned, Chanel cashmere twinset, navy slim-fitting Gucci pants, and pale suede Bruno Magli loafers.

Perfect taste, perfect measurements; that was Lavinia Thurston, duchess of Louster. *Perfect, perfect, perfect! Can we not find something less boring?* Lavinia's question echoed in Sarah's mind, and she sighed, picturing her brother married to the duchess. It was true—Lavinia was faultless in every way, from her complexion from heaven to her elegant hands and slim fingers, the fashionably squared nails buffed and polished in a French manicure.

She was classically beautiful. She was exceptionally rich. At nineteen years of age, the duchess of Louster had it all. And in Sarah's opinion it was all too predictable a choice for Viscount Maxwell Pennington. Too . . . *boring!*

"No, thank you. I'm afraid this will not do," Lavinia said frostily but politely in her impeccable elocution-trained accent.

Sarah couldn't help groaning out loud as Lavinia waved another fashion-consultant minion away and turned up her nose at a fourth minion, who was busily explaining how if it would please the duchess, they could easily have some Belgian peasants from the world-renowned peasant town of wherever hand stitch an exquisite lace dress or embroider and bead a twenty-foot train with gold silk from India and miniature pearls from Japan.

So much for shopping! Sarah sniffed. *This is worse than a picnic at a power plant!*

Sarah scowled as Lavinia looked like she was about to cry, lifting her trembling left hand to her eyes, her third finger flashing with the pear-shaped white-diamond-and-emerald engagement ring that Max had given her.

Ordinarily a day of shopping that included a visit to the oh-so-hoity-toity couturier to the royals, the House of Vervier, would have bucked up Sarah's day considerably. An afternoon that included the prospect of a slew of good purchases and then perhaps a scone-and-cream tea at Harrods . . . it ought never to be turned down. But Lavinia had a way of spoiling everything.

Granted, I'm not perfectly behaved, Sarah admitted as Lavinia folded her slender arms and looked pained, a tiny frown creasing her alabaster skin as she surveyed a sketch Jean-Yves Vervier himself handed her. *But I'm not this bad!*

Sarah could tolerate people having the odd fit

from time to time. She herself did it often enough. But what she loathed about Lavinia was the fact that she walked around with her nose permanently tilted in the air, always looking like she knew she was better than everyone else. She never broke down or screamed or shouted, but somehow this made her worse in Sarah's eyes. More of a hypocrite. Like now. Lavinia was as close to a breakdown as Lavinia could get, yet the most emotion Lavinia ever betrayed was in her whining. Or her slight, sniffling cry, which she could activate whenever it suited her. Because underneath her whinging and whining, underneath her cool reserve, lurked a coldly manipulative schemer who always got what she wanted. Yes, Sarah was hip to that part of Lavinia too, even if her brother couldn't see it. . . .

Oh, brace up, would you! Sarah longed to shout as Lavinia, looking like she'd just swallowed a tub of arsenic, curtly—yet at the same time using code words of politeness—asked Vervier to show her something else. It wasn't that Sarah felt sorry for poofy, poncey Vervier or any of the scuttling serfs around Lavinia, but truly, Lavinia was being an awful stick-in-the-mud. Hardly like a bride-to-be. It was altogether thoroughly depressing.

"Why not get married in a mini?" Sarah quipped, trying to lighten the mood before Lavinia lost it completely. "What about a bloodred mini and a rhinestone tiara? Sort of trashy glam, Courtney Love style?" Sarah giggled, but instead of even cracking a smile at the joke, Lavinia stiffly ignored her and ordered someone to bring her a cup of tea and give her some "breathing room."

"What a hateful selection!" Lavinia remarked to Sarah, flopping onto a mint green divan as the management rushed off to attend to the tea. "This place is going downhill."

Like this day, Sarah thought. At first she'd tried her best to rev up Lavinia and get into the spirit of things, from offering opinions and advice to desperate joke cracking, but nothing had helped. Lavinia had remained sullen and bloodless no matter how many stunning fabrics were held up to her flawless face, no matter how many cooing compliments coated the air around her. No matter that she was supposed to be excited and in love!

"I honestly can't picture myself in any of those atrocious fabrics." Lavinia sighed, her eyes glazed and empty looking. "Seriously, Sarah, this could turn out to be a complete and utter disaster!"

A twinge of pity snaked through Sarah as she saw the unhappiness and boredom reflected in Lavinia's eyes. Nobody should look so miserable at their wedding fitting! Sarah also couldn't help feeling a flash of regret that she and Lavinia couldn't be close. After all, both of them were young; both of them had expensive tastes. Both had lost their mothers at a young age. And Lavinia's father had died too. *That in some ways should make her a deeper person,* Sarah thought. *She's been through a lot.* . . .

Yet if Lavinia had been through anything, it didn't show either in the way she acted or in the way she looked. And no matter how nice it would be for Max, Sarah knew that she and Lavinia would never be like sisters. Lavinia was too much like a robot, and when she wasn't being robotically perfect, then she was being a coldly disdainful snob. And all in her perfectly chilly, subtle way.

"I think I'll have to go to Paris." Lavinia sniffed, blanching at the thought, as if she were planning a trip to prison. "Perhaps the Parisians can do better." Her lip quivered as she absently twisted a sapphire bracelet on her slim wrist.

"Hmmph," Sarah responded, gulping her tea as if it were a magic potion that could help her grow wings so she could fly out of there. *God forbid I should look so glum when I'm being fitted for my wedding!*

But Sarah knew that would never happen. If she were getting married, she would look anything but frigid. Of course, she would wear something befitting a noblewoman, but she wouldn't act like one, all cool and feeble and dull, like Lavinia.

141

Because I would be in love . . . , Sarah thought dreamily, picturing herself at Vervier, selecting a sleeveless white bias-cut silk dress, accented perhaps by a tiny bit of embroidery at the hem, Nick's engagement ring on her finger—maybe a baguette-cut diamond surrounded by tiny cabochon rubies. Something modern and stylish but also classic . . .

Or even a cheap gold band if that was all Nick could afford. Sarah could live with that. If it was Nick's ring, then that was all that mattered.

Sarah pictured herself hopping up and down, hugging scrawny Jean-Yves Vervier himself. In love with love.

That was exactly how she'd be because she'd be marrying Nick, and so their wedding and everything around it would be an expression of their love. . . .

Expression of our love! Suddenly Sarah froze while at the same time she felt a deep, fiery blush rising up through her chest and neck as she considered the words and their possible meaning in the light of Nick's recent proposition.

Sarah swallowed hard. She still hadn't given Nick an answer about whether she was ready to make love to him. And she realized she *also* still hadn't gotten any further with her decision making. In fact, for most of the day she'd managed to put it out of her mind. She'd been distracted by school, her fight with her father, Lavinia.

Beep, beep! With shaky hands Sarah returned her bone-thin teacup clattering to its saucer, her pulse leaping and quickening. She fished through her school blazer's pockets, fumbling for her cell phone. It was probably Nick now, calling to ask her what she'd decided.

Or maybe Daddy, calling to tell me he's sending me to reform school for aristocrats! Sarah mused darkly, snapping open her cell phone.

"Guess who, angel girl!"

"Nick!" Though she was nervous to hear his voice, relief and excitement also swelled through Sarah at the sound of it. "How's the girl bonding?" Nick chuckled.

"Not. Happening," Sarah muttered, grimly emphasizing each word, her eyes on Lavinia, who sat so rigidly, she looked like she was posing for her portrait. "Honestly, I feel like I might keel over and *die* if I stay here one more minute," she whispered.

"Well, then, how about I cheer you up? Can you try to meet me later tonight?" Nick asked. "At the park, nine P.M.? I'll be there with Simon and Fiona."

"I can't!" Sarah replied hoarsely. "You know I'm grounded," she added. "Besides, Max's pal

James is coming to supper, and Daddy's insisting I put in a proper appearance. Thank God he's letting me bring Victoria," she chattered. "At least I'll have an ally during dinner."

"Dad's trying to marry you off, is he?" Nick queried, and Sarah felt her blush deepen, rising up to inflame her cheeks.

"Gosh, n-no . . . um," she stammered, embarrassed and apologetic that she'd mentioned stupid James at all. She knew it would only make Nick feel worse after the way her father had dismissed him so shoddily and refused to let him see Sarah.

"Just a joke," Nick broke in gruffly, and Sarah felt ashamed and thankful. Trust Nick to make her feel better. *Yet another thing I love about him . . .*

"Look, just try to be there, can't you? Give it a shot. Even if you come late," Nick pleaded.

"Well . . ." Sarah trailed off doubtfully, watching as bored, impassive Lavinia reapplied a coat of sheer gloss to her lips and picked a piece of lint off her sweater. "I . . . can't," she finished lamely, heaving a big sigh. "I wish, but I don't see it happening."

"Pity." Nick sounded so disappointed, and Sarah wished fervently she could be with him right now so she could throw her arms around him. It had to be hard on him going out with her, a girl with such a strict, complicated family obsessed with rules and traditions.

"Well, then you need to figure out a way for us to be together this weekend," Nick replied urgently. "Please, Sarah, else I'll really freak from not seeing you!"

"I'll—I'll try," Sarah responded weakly, a pins-and-needles kind of feeling tingling in her legs as she pictured what Nick meant by "together." "I'll talk to you soon," she murmured, still of two minds as she slowly pressed end call on her cell phone and slipped it back into her pocket. *Together.* She and Nick. Making love. Their bodies as close as two bodies can get . . .

It was thrilling and tantalizing and amazing to think about something that exciting after a cold helping of Iced Lavinia.

But it was also scary. And there was no getting around the fact that once a girl lost her virginity, she could never get it back. If she did it, Sarah knew she would be going down a one-way street. And she was no closer to figuring out whether she was ready for that one-way street or not.

Should I take it slow? Sarah wondered, wishing she could ask Lavinia's advice, even though she knew Lavinia would only stare blankly and tell her something stupid, something like, "You might as well get it over with." Or, "Lie back and think of England!"

Perhaps she should take it slow—wait a while

145

until she was sure she could handle it. *Yes,* Sarah thought, resolved now, feeling suddenly like she'd made some progress in her thinking. *I'll take it slow.*

Or on second thought, perhaps it was time to let her fears go . . .

"James!"

As he pulled his red Alfa Romeo Spider to a sharp stop in front of Pennington House, crunching gravel beneath the tires, twenty-one-year-old James Leer held up his hand and waved at Max, who had come out of the house to greet him.

"Hello there!" James grinned, removing his Ray-Ban sunglasses and then gripping Max's outstretched hand for a shake. "What's potting?"

"Not much." Max shrugged cheerfully, chewing on an apple. "Supposed to be nailing the thesis, but can't say I've got much done."

Though he was almost six-foot-two, James jumped nimbly out of the sports car and clapped Max on the back. "Me either," he confessed as they walked toward the house in the darkening evening light.

Like Max, like James, James said to himself, smiling as he thought of how similar they were. Growing up on adjacent estates and being the same age, the two had been lifelong best friends and had done almost everything side by side, from school at Eton to university at Oxford. The fact that neither was using the study break to work was just further evidence of how like-minded they were.

Not that either of them was particularly slack in their academic habits. In fact, as James neared completion of his degree and internship as an investment-banking trainee, he found himself growing more and more eager to get out of university and make a name for himself in the world of finance.

But the past few days he'd found it difficult to concentrate. *Maybe it's anticipation?* he asked himself, greeting Mary as she ushered him into the foyer of Pennington. Anticipation could be what had broken his focus. Anticipation of the dinner at Pennington.

Anticipation of seeing a certain Vanessa Shaw . . .

"Lovely to see you, Mary," James said warmly as Mary beamed at him and patted him on the shoulder. *Dear old Mary . . .* James had known Mary practically all of his life. "Nice to see you too, Alice," he added, looking over Mary's shoulder in time to see mousy Alice glowing red from his compliment and ducking her head shyly.

It *was* nice to see them all. James was very fond of the Penningtons and their staff. The earl was rather a good bloke despite his codgerly nobleman ways. Lord Pennington was in fact very similar to James's own father, who wasn't an aristocrat but an upperclassman of great wealth, and so the Penningtons and the Leers occupied the same echelon of society. But though James was pleased to see Max and Mary and looked forward to seeing the earl, there was one person James wanted to see more than any of them. And the only one at Pennington, he knew, who had no interest in seeing him.

"Looking for someone?" Max teased with a knowing smile. "Extra glad to be invited over to dinner *chez nous?*" he added jokingly.

"You know me. Can't pass up an opportunity for self-torture," James replied wryly, scanning the foyer and parlor with his light gray-blue eyes, looking for a sign of Vanessa.

James had confessed his agonizingly huge crush on Vanessa to Max, who'd been all for it and offered to do whatever he could to make it easy for James to be in her company.

But Max knew as well as James did that Vanessa hadn't the slightest interest in him. Several dinners and lunches at the house had proved exactly that. No matter how many times James had tried to engage Vanessa in conversation or even tried to exchange simple pleasantries, she avoided him as if he had leprosy.

But watch me come back for more! James chastised himself as he sank his long frame into a leather couch in the parlor. Why did he come back for more? It was bad enough seeing the disinterest in Vanessa's lovely, guarded eyes the first time round, but now it had gotten to the point where Vanessa clearly knew James was interested in her, and so it was all the more crushing to endure her cold-shoulder avoidance.

"Darts?" Max broke into James's thoughts, grabbing a fistful of darts from the dartboard.

"Why not? I could use the stress reliever." James unconsciously clenched and unclenched the tiny muscle in his prominent jaw, running a hand through his fine, wheat blond hair. He'd had his hair cut earlier that day and taken extra care to wear a nice shirt that night. Nice, but not too formal, in case Vanessa thought he was uncool. A gray, fifties-style knit shirt that his brother's wife had told him brought out the color of his eyes. *Fat lot of good that'll do me, though!* James thought in frustration, throwing his dart extra hard. *I could be wearing a neon jumpsuit, and she wouldn't even know I existed!*

"Good shot, Leer. Bull's-eye!" Max commended James, admiring the arrow that punctured the dartboard's black-and-red center circle. "Rejection's really helped your game," he added with a chuckle.

"Sorry, mate, but I couldn't resist. You look like someone just threw a dart at *you*."

Give her time and I'm sure she would, James thought blackly, furrowing his brow in concentration as he aimed another dart and thought of the last time he'd seen Vanessa, when he'd stopped in for a Sunday lunch. She'd studiously managed to avoid looking him in the eye throughout the meal. And when after dessert James had finally managed to get Vanessa to talk to him by asking her about herself, she'd replied monosyllabically, her voice as frosty as the lemon sherbet she'd spooned into his bowl.

Whunk! Bull's-eye again.

But rather than feeling pleased at his good aim, James merely shrugged at his score and resettled on the couch, keeping a careful eye out in case Vanessa happened to be passing nearby.

"She *is* working tonight," Max said as he extended an arm for aim and then threw his dart. "So remember your table manners," he ribbed, before swearing under his breath as he checked his dart, which had missed the bull's-eye by a hair.

James flushed slightly, shifting self-consciously on the couch. It was decent of Max to look into his plight, and James knew his best pal had only good intentions, but somehow James doubted that Max really understood what it was like to be interested in someone who treated you like horse manure.

Granted, Lavinia wasn't the warmest presence in the world, and she and Max certainly didn't act like lovebirds, but James knew Lavinia cared for Max, in her way. And everything was all planned out. A wedding in six months. All in all, a vastly different scenario from James's own love life.

Quit the self-pity, Leer! James ordered himself, suddenly annoyed that he could feel so utterly gloomy over a girl. But Vanessa was no ordinary girl. James had never seen anyone as beautiful as her before, and he couldn't help it: When he fell, he fell hard.

"Aperitif?" Max held up a crystal decanter of sherry and grabbed two glasses with his free hand. "I know it's slightly early, but you could probably use it. Before the torture begins," he added with a grin.

James exhaled with a groan, part pity, part self-mocking. And then he laughed. It truly *was* humorous. The rich kid next door coming over to be humiliated by the neighbors' servant girl. Humiliating and also oddly funny. "Yeah, I'll take a shot," he replied. "Make it a double."

Max was right. James did feel the need for a drink to dull his senses before Vanessa made her appearance. Casting another none-too-furtive, longing look at the parlor door, James downed the sherry in one gulp, knowing that when Vanessa did materialize, he'd be in for some serious ego bashing.

But despite the thought of Vanessa's reluctant appearance in the dining room and the wordless insults she would manage to convey with her body language—even then, seeing Vanessa was still a thrill to look forward to.

I'll take what I can get, James mused philosophically, because there was no question: A sullen Vanessa, in James's opinion, was still infinitely better than no Vanessa at all.

Chapter
Eight

"Might I have a few more rolls?" Max said politely into the intercom. He wasn't wildly hungry, and after the fantastic rack of lamb, new potatoes, and creamed spinach that Cook had prepared for the entrée, bread was the last thing he needed.

But Max made the request for another reason, the reason walking toward him right now, smiling and holding a basket of rolls. Elizabeth, the new scullery maid.

"Marvelous to have you round again, eh, James," the earl boomed, halting Max's thought flow. "We haven't seen much of you since you started your investment-banking internship."

"Yes, sir," James replied. "Very glad to see you again, sir. And always glad to sample Matilda's cooking."

"Oxford kitchens still awful, are they?"

And so they bantered on. Max admired his friend for looking so bright and cheery, but he knew the chap was rather disappointed inside. Vanessa had avoided the serving all night. Which was great for Max—who got to have the pleasure of Elizabeth's presence—but rather tough on James.

But for all of James's frustration, Max envied him. James was filthy rich and from a top-notch old London society family, but he wasn't nobility and so could ask out anyone he chose. . . . *He could ask Elizabeth out if he wanted to,* Max mused, warming as Elizabeth flashed her dazzling smile at him. Max smiled back, holding her gaze for a moment as he thought back to their lovely chance meeting in the gardens earlier. The way they'd fallen into such an easy conversation that he'd felt like they'd known each other for ages . . .

"Thank you, Elizabeth," Lord Pennington said sharply, eyeing Max meaningfully as Elizabeth demurely slipped away, moving down the table to attend to Sarah, who suddenly demanded bread herself.

That was uncalled for! Max returned his father's steely gaze, feeling a sudden, uncharacteristically strong anger come over him. How dare his father talk to Elizabeth in such an abrasive tone! And who was he to stare Max down in that way, monitoring whom he smiled at, for God's sake?

I am my own man, Max thought angrily. But at the same time Max knew that wasn't entirely true. He was his father's son living in his father's home. And his father's way of doing things ruled. That was just how it was. How it had always been.

Looking over at his father, Max felt again a familiar kind of desperation churning inside him. It wasn't that his father was a bad chap. But he was woefully out of tune with the times, and Max wished fervently that he could just tell his father to stay out of his affairs. But that would never fly. The earl kept close tabs on his children and refused to stay out of their affairs. Like now. With mounting embarrassment Max watched as his father tried to get conversation going between James and Sarah.

"Sarah's got a good head for numbers," Lord Pennington told James, gesturing with his fork at Sarah, who'd been giggling and chatting with her friend Victoria all through the meal, uninterested in joining in the table conversation. "I think perhaps she might end up interested in finance. Maybe you could give her some tips on how to approach the arena, James," the earl babbled on, and Max winced. His father was being so obvious, trying to get James and Sarah to chat. It was really quite an awkward situation all round.

"What rubbish, Daddy." Sarah spoke up suddenly, her eyes glittering with annoyance. "I'm useless at maths. And I'd rather die than be a banker! It sounds dead boring!"

"That's right, Lord P. She came stone last in the test last week," Victoria added emphatically, bobbing her head of springy red curls as Sarah left the table to intercom for more iced water.

James laughed nervously as Sarah reseated herself, glaring at her father. For his part the earl looked quite displeased, shooting Sarah a warning look. "Perhaps if you applied yourself a bit more to your studies instead of engaging in other *extracurricular* activities, you might develop your skills, my girl," he added forcefully.

To which Sarah rolled her eyes and then stood up from the table. "You're quite right, Daddy," she said evenly, pulling at Victoria's sleeve. "Which is why I simply must excuse myself and Victoria here. We have an exam tomorrow, and we've still got a lot of swatting left."

Bloody hell, Max thought, flashing James a silent apology. Between his father and his sister the evening was quite obviously sliding downhill fast. There was only one forgivable thing about the dinner hour, Max decided. And it was the few minutes of grace provided by Elizabeth.

As Max watched Elizabeth leave the dining

room, he couldn't help noting how exceptionally beautiful she was. Even in her simple oxford-shirt-and-khaki-pants uniform, her fabulous blond hair tied back primly with a navy ribbon, Elizabeth was a knockout.

Oh, man! With a jolt of recognition Max suddenly realized he was in trouble. He hadn't really given it proper thought, but as he watched Elizabeth disappear through the doors, he knew there was no denying it.

For the first time since he'd met Lavinia, he was interested—*truly* interested—in another girl.

Not good for someone about to be married.

Not good at all . . . Max felt a flash of guilt combined with a sense of gnawing unease.

He pushed away his plate. He'd lost his appetite.

"Thank the pope! We've made our great escape!" Sarah exclaimed with relief, hurling herself onto her bed exultantly. "What a wretched meal!"

"I thought the nosh was rather good," Victoria replied mildly, thumbing through an issue of *British Mademoiselle* as she settled cross-legged on Sarah's Persian carpet, next to the crackling fire that burned in the hearth. "Pity I stuffed my face at lunch; else I'd have had seconds for dinner. . . ."

"Not the food, Vicks," Sarah retorted crossly, vigorously filing her nails. "My *father!* I'm just

157

glad we managed to excuse ourselves from having to sit through the dessert hour. Another minute and I swear I'd have lost my marbles."

Sarah shook her head, relieved that her father hadn't put up a fuss when she'd abruptly decided to exit before the entrée was over with. But it was really all too much, more than Sarah could stand. And even if she hadn't gorged herself on a fish-and-chip lunch at school, watching her father trying to maneuver her toward James would have ruined Sarah's normally healthy appetite.

"It's utterly nauseating!" Sarah declared in disgust, slashing emphatically at the air with her nail file. "I'm not some prize mare needing to be paired up with a stallion, but that's how it feels!" She hurled herself back on her pillows and stared miserably at the ceiling. "Honestly, Vic, I feel quite, quite ill!"

"Oh, come on," Victoria retorted cheerfully, and Sarah frowned. She'd expected her best friend in the whole world to at least commiserate with her, but Victoria looked unfazed, flipping through the magazine, her round, dimpled face relaxed and smiling. "James is a dream boat," she continued, her hazel eyes twinkling mischievously. "Who cares if it's a setup?"

"*I* care!" Sarah shot back vehemently, her eyes blazing. "Vic, have you forgotten that I already have a boyfriend?"

"Really? I didn't know that!" Victoria jibed good-naturedly, tossing the magazine at Sarah. "How come you never talk about him?" she teased, and Sarah had to crack a smile. It was true—she did spend her entire life eating, breathing, and obsessing over Nick. *But I'm in love!* Sarah reasoned to herself. Which was what made her father's insidious attempts to set her up with James all the more odious.

But her father wasn't the only problem, and Sarah sighed as she revisited the conundrum that had been spinning around in her head all day. She still hadn't made her decision. Couldn't make her decision. And the more she thought about it, the more she fretted over it.

". . . I'm just not sure I'm ready to lose my virginity," Sarah explained as she finished re-unloading her problem onto Victoria for the second time that day. "But if I don't, I'm scared Nick will leave me for some other girl," she admitted gloomily as Victoria listened patiently, painting her fingernails with Sarah's ruby red Goth Glam, a fashionable and expensive new nail polish from New York.

"Oh, come on!" Victoria burst out at last, almost smudging her nails. "If Nick really loved you, he wouldn't dump you just so he could sleep with some slut!"

Victoria did have a point, Sarah had to concede.

But Victoria was also a virgin and would say whatever she needed to convince Sarah not to have sex. *Because she's never been in love, so she doesn't know what love feels like!* Sarah reasoned. And maybe Victoria simply didn't want Sarah to do something she hadn't done. *Or maybe she's just looking out for me . . .*

Sarah shook her head gloomily. This sex question and everything that surrounded it was all one big riddle, one big stalemate, one big dead end. No matter which way she leaned, there were arguments for leaning in the opposite direction.

". . . You could get *diseases,* for goodness' sake," Victoria nattered on, rattling off a list of nasties, her nose scrunched in fear and disgust. "And there's pregnancy, of course."

"Hello? Haven't you ever heard of condoms?" Sarah shot back, rolling her eyes.

"They're not foolproof, you know," Victoria retorted. "Remember Judy Newton from—"

"Vic!" Sarah sighed and held up a hand. "I *know* all of that," she retorted, swiping the nail polish from Victoria. "But I also know that I'm in love with Nick. Sex isn't all bad, you know!" she continued, dabbing a blob of polish on her thumbnail. "Besides, it's pointless even discussing this," Sarah added bitterly. "How am I supposed to know if I'm ready for sex if I can't even see Nick! And as if being grounded isn't bad enough, my dad's threatening to home school me!"

"Raw deal," Victoria admitted sympathetically. "We've got to make a plan to get Lord P. off your back," she reflected. "Otherwise you might as well declare your teen life over and join a convent. . . ."

But as the girls began to brainstorm back and forth, Sarah felt a well of hopelessness expanding inside her, growing bigger and bigger. Her father was too angry to sweet-talk, and Sarah couldn't think of a single way to twist his arm and change his mind about grounding her. *I'm doomed!* she thought in defeat. *My life is over!*

"Unless . . ." Victoria's eyes lit up, and her full mouth stretched slowly into a wide smile.

"What? Unless what?" Sarah practically shouted, almost knocking the nail polish onto her lily-white bedspread.

"Unless you convince your dad that you're into James," Victoria suggested. "Flirt with him, play interested. That way your dad will relax. He knows James is a total gentleman and won't try to lure you into any unseemly, improper situations."

"Plus he wants me to go for a guy like James," Sarah added thoughtfully, beginning to cotton to Victoria's plan. "If I act like I'm into James, Dad will be pleased as punch."

"Then maybe he'll ease up on you and stop

watching you like a hawk!" Victoria continued, grinning. "He'll think you've got this safe, cute, Little Miss Innocence crush on a guy he approves of . . . and you're home free!"

"Brilliant!" Sarah squealed, bounding off her bed. "If Dad thinks I'm on the right path, he'll stop worrying and give me more freedom . . . *to see Nick!*" she erupted triumphantly.

The plan was watertight. Sarah could barely contain the excitement that coursed through her veins at the prospect of changing her awful situation. All she had to do was flirt with James. *Easy peasy pie!* Sarah thought happily, clapping. And flirting with James would be totally harmless. Sarah knew there was no danger of James getting all flustered over her and embarrassing them both. *He's so smitten with Vanessa, he'll barely even notice me!*

The plan was genius. Now all that remained was the execution. *And then I'll have my life back!*

"Right on, Vic." Sarah high-fived her pal, and then the two girls headed for the door. Almost sprinting to the dining room, Sarah was unable to contain the grin that spread across her face, the first genuinely happy smile of her day. *Seems I have room for dessert after all!*

Oh, Lord! Vanessa heaved a pained sigh as she shook icing sugar over a Black Forest gâteau and

162

placed the cake on a silver plate, surrounding it with miniature puffed meringues, baked earlier in the day. Vanessa had been dawdling, taking her time over the whole process, but she knew she had to get in there with dessert sooner or later.

So far she'd managed to avoid dealing directly with the family, relying on Elizabeth to do the serving while Vanessa remained in the kitchen and helped prepare the plates and clean up. But Cook had ordered Elizabeth to begin mopping. Which meant that Vanessa had to endure dessert. *Make that endure James Leer leering at me like* I'm *dessert!*

Setting her mouth into a disinterested, somewhat sour line, Vanessa prepared to take in the sweets. In fairness, James Leer wasn't the leering type, despite his name, she grudgingly admitted to herself. He was quite good-looking, a gentleman, and had decent manners. Still, the guy was so obvious, it drove Vanessa berserk.

From the very first moment that James had spotted her, he hadn't taken his eyes off her. Every time he came around, it was the same thing. Puppy-dog eyes filled with longing.

And Vanessa was so not in the mood for that look. *It's bad enough having to serve that bunch of prigs,* she thought angrily as she lifted the dessert tray. *But now I have to contend with the minimogul from next door! Ugh!*

As she walked into the dining room, Vanessa purposefully avoided looking at James, though she could feel his intent gaze boring into her like a drill.

Vanessa hated James. It was nothing personal; she simply hated him because of who he was and what he represented. The way Vanessa saw it, just as the upper classes looked down on the commoners because of who they were by birth, so too the commoners could loathe the upper classes purely because of their class. It went both ways.

Not your fault, Vanessa thought coolly as she traipsed past James to the buffet table. *You're just born that way!* James was cute, with his blond hair and muscular body, and perhaps if he worked as a fireman or a bartender, then Vanessa would hate him less. Maybe even let him buy her a beer. *But then again, maybe not . . .*

"The . . . cake looks lovely," James spluttered awkwardly as Vanessa plunged the cake knife into the gâteau and sliced away matter-of-factly.

I didn't make it, so stop salivating over me! Vanessa was dying to quip, but of course she simply kept her lips pressed together, hoping her silence could speak volumes.

"I'd like a meringue, please, Vanessa," the earl announced, holding his plate up to Vanessa.

It took sheer willpower to not grab his plate

and drop it on the floor, but Vanessa responded with a sullen, "Yes, milord," and dolefully did her duty.

Inside, of course, Vanessa was seething. Seething with rage against them all, from Sarah and her fat twit of a friend what's-her-face, to Max, to the earl. And especially James for all his adoration and tongue-tied reverence. Couldn't the guy take a hint? Couldn't he tell that Vanessa wasn't the girl of his dreams, that in fact she didn't have anything for him to be moony about?

Apparently not. Vanessa could still feel James's eyes on her back. And she knew James hadn't yet had his fill. He would no doubt ring for her with some made-up excuse or another once she'd left the dining room. All of which drove her up the wall. *Yes, you can have my service at the ring of an intercom,* she thought angrily, wishing she could voice her opinion, *but that is all you're getting!*

That and of course a rude surprise once I get my hands on some proof . . . Vanessa shoveled meringues onto Sarah and Max's plates, a faraway look in her eyes as she pictured their faces contorted in horror once she announced who she was and what a scummy excuse for both a father and an aristocrat Lord Pennington was.

I'll do it right here, Vanessa fantasized, picturing herself being ordered to dish up dessert and instead dishing up dirt on her lord and master! Now, *that* would be sweet!

But first things first . . . Vanessa picked up pace, hurriedly depositing plates in front of the girls and Max and then finally, reluctantly, depositing a plate in front of the almost drooling James. It wasn't just that she wanted to get out of there fast so as to avoid more of James's lovey-dovey stares. Vanessa had extra motivation to get things moving along.

Because the sooner she served, the sooner they ate. The sooner they ate, the sooner she could get out of there and get on with her evening plans.

And Vanessa wanted that desperately. It would be tough to get into the countess's suite that night, what with the whole family being home for the evening, but Vanessa was certainly prepared to give it a shot. Exposing the earl's hypocrisy was incentive enough, but James's drooling over her gave Vanessa the added push.

*I will *get out of here,* she vowed silently. *But not before I take this family down!*

Chapter Nine

Stop staring, you stupid git! James reprimanded himself, feeling his pulse zoom into overdrive as Vanessa glided into the family room, bearing a tray of coffee. But James couldn't help it. Throughout dessert he'd been painfully aware of Vanessa's presence around him and utterly transfixed by her beauty. Even in her uniform she looked like a fashion model. *And in her expression too,* James observed wryly, thinking of how well Vanessa would fit in, sneering on a Paris runway.

James forced himself to look away from Vanessa, taking in the scene around him instead. Everyone was settled comfortably in the family room—the earl watching the CNN evening news on television, Max setting up a backgammon game, and even the girls had come down from Sarah's room to have coffee and liqueur chocolates and were giggling in the corner.

But James preferred to watch Vanessa pouring the coffee. Or rather, he couldn't avoid watching her. His eyes just involuntarily tracked her, and he had to keep reminding himself to look away.

You're embarrassing yourself as usual! James continued with his internal diatribe as he stole another shy glance at Vanessa. He wished his crush wasn't so stupefyingly obvious, but James couldn't help it. He wore his heart on his sleeve. *That's just who I am,* he thought with a sigh. *Not the subtlest bloke in the book!*

"Just ask her out," Max murmured, and James tore his eyes away from Vanessa's back for a second to respond to his friend's outrageous suggestion. "What's stopping you?"

"Are you off your rocker?" James muttered back as Max shook dice onto the backgammon board. "The girl loathes me! I'd just get rejected."

"Well, at least you're optimistic," Max ribbed. "That always helps."

"I also don't think it's very polite to put Vanessa in a position like that," James continued in a low voice. "I mean, it's clear she doesn't like me, so asking her out would just be . . . tacky. Disrespectful."

"I still think—," Max argued, but James cut him off with a warning.

"She's coming," he hissed urgently as Vanessa appeared, holding two cups of coffee.

God, she's beautiful, James thought longingly as Vanessa handed him his coffee. Up close, Vanessa was too pretty to look at, and James quickly looked away. But not before he saw the disdain in her brown eyes. Disdain and something else too. *Defiance.*

Got my answer right there, James thought gloomily. In case there had been any doubt, Vanessa's eyes told him all he needed to know. *If I asked her out, she'd probably spray me with kitchen bleach!*

Why did he do this to himself? As Vanessa stalked off, all James could do was groan. Liking her was torture, wanting her was hell. But there was nothing he *could* do. Vanessa was so stunning, she'd captivated him from the word go. It was just chemistry, and James was fully, completely caught in a hormonal grip. Of course he would love to spare himself this embarrassment, but what choice did he have? The woman was the spitting image of Audrey Hepburn. And how could he resist his own heart?

All these thoughts raced through James's head as he played a disinterested game of backgammon with Max and attempted to talk himself out of his hopeless crush on Vanessa. But the problem was, James knew his attraction to her wasn't simply skin-deep. There was more to it than that. More to Vanessa than that.

Everything about Vanessa spelled independence and free will. She radiated a kind of grit and edginess that came through in her manner, from her confident walk to the supercilious arch of her eyebrows. She might be just a kitchen maid, but Vanessa wasn't one to be controlled by anyone. And James admired her for it.

But why does she dismiss me so readily? James thought as Vanessa disappeared through the door, leaving the family to their coffee. *Why won't she give me the time of day?* It wasn't that James thought he was such a catch, nor was he particularly any kind of ladies' man, but he still found it odd that Vanessa wouldn't even give him a chance and had seemed to loathe him on sight.

The one logical and good reason for ignoring a chap would be if one were already taken. But Max had canvassed the scene and reported that he didn't think Vanessa had a boyfriend. So that probably wasn't it. There had to be another reason why Vanessa couldn't bear to be in James's company.

I'm supposedly good-looking, James thought, deliberating over his tall, athletic frame, regular features, blue-gray eyes, and blond hair. He'd never thought of himself as particularly attractive and didn't trust himself to judge that kind of thing. But he'd been told often enough that he was good-looking. *So if the odds are that she doesn't find me hideously ugly, then why is she so revolted by me?* James wondered, going through a list of other things that should have made him desirable. For one, he had gobs of family money. For two, he wasn't a layabout, and therefore Vanessa could respect him for his own ambitions, for the fact that though he could easily have rested on his laurels and spent his father's estate, James had worked like a demon to get an internship in investment banking. It hadn't been handed to him on a plate, and James didn't take his opportunities for granted. *So why does she find me so offensive?*

"You know what your problem is, James?" Max piped up suddenly, as if tuning in to his thought waves.

"What?" James was all ears, desperate for any tips he could get.

"You're too nice. Nice guys finish last," Max said, leaning back into his chair and appraising James critically, his head cocked.

"Look who's talking," James answered with a snort. "Since when are you the bad boy?"

"Never. But I'm not interested in the Blair Witch over there," Max replied, nodding in the direction of Vanessa, who had returned to pour the earl a fresh cup of coffee.

James considered Max's words as he glanced at Vanessa. And then surprisingly, without warning, Vanessa suddenly looked over at him! James felt his stomach turn in a sickening, wrenching anticipation of her scowl, but Vanessa didn't scowl or sneer. She just pulled a Mona Lisa. She looked totally enigmatic. Unreadable.

What makes her tick? James wondered. Nothing about Vanessa made sense. Just the fact that she'd work as a kitchen maid was weird when clearly she could do anything she wanted and had the confidence to make it happen. That much was obvious from even one look at Vanessa. She could be a model or an actress, for starters. Yet here she was, working as a Pennington servant. It was nothing short of unfathomable.

In fact, the whole situation was ridiculous, and James couldn't help wondering what his parents would make of his attachment to the Penningtons' scullery maid. *They wouldn't be pleased,* James realized, his features hardening into a grim half smile at the thought of his prim and proper mum and his by-the-book, old-school dad. But at the same time James knew his parents would eventually come round if he ever managed to get Vanessa to be his girlfriend. The Leers were traditionalists, but they had also raised James to think for himself. *They'd get over it,* he thought, and then immediately wondered why he was even bothering to go there. Vanessa could hardly manage to look at him, much less go out with him!

"Girls, keep it down!" the earl roared, turning up the volume on the TV as Sarah and Victoria stifled shrieks in the corner, evidently highly amused by something.

James turned back to his backgammon game, feeling defeated in his games of the heart. *Might as well win something tonight!* he thought miserably, shaking up the dice.

Two ones. A hopelessly low score. "Bollocks," James muttered under his breath. "A born loser . . ."

"I'm telling you, Leer, it's all about attitude," Max encouraged, hunching over so as not to be overheard. "Vanessa's a bit of a spitfire. You're too polite and low-key for her. That's why she's annoyed by you. You're a mouse, and she's a cat. It's too easy for her to destroy you."

"That helps!" James groaned, running a hand through his hair. "I can't change who I am!"

"That's where you're wrong," Max replied cheerfully. "Listen," he murmured. "It's just a question of tweaking your approach. Be more assertive. Ask her out. I'm telling you, she'd have a heck of a lot more respect for you if you met her head-on instead of shrinking away."

"Hmmm." James was silent for a moment. He had to admit, what Max said made some sense. Perhaps Vanessa *would* respect him if he were more assertive. *So do it,* his inner voice suddenly commanded, and James was surprised by himself. He was normally much more tentative. *And where has that got you?* the voice prompted. Another good point.

Yes, James thought, feeling his heart begin to hammer at his chest. *You need to be direct. Ask her out!*

"What have you got to lose?" Max added, and James nodded. He didn't have anything left to lose. Pride? That was already on the floor, and Vanessa had stomped all over it. There was only one thing left to do.

"Okay," James said, his voice firm. He stood up then and purposefully strode across the room to where Vanessa stood. She'd brought the Black Forest cake into the parlor and was now arranging a clean stack of plates next to a tray of Cointreau liqueur chocolates.

Here goes, James thought, taking a deep breath as Vanessa eyed him moving toward her.

But just as James neared Vanessa and opened his mouth, hoping to formulate a polite yet confident request to perhaps "have a coffee sometime," he was intercepted by a small hand on his forearm.

"Jamesy!"

James turned to see Sarah, her cheeks oddly pink, her eyes glittering. "We've barely chatted all evening!" Sarah exclaimed. "And you still haven't told me about your hotshot internship," she gushed, threading her arm around his and pulling him over toward the couch. "Do let's sit and natter for a bit!"

Odd, James thought as he dutifully and reluctantly followed Sarah. Teenagers were a peculiar lot. Especially teenage girls. Totally flighty and supremely unpredictable—one moment they ignored you, the next they were all over you. Ruining your one chance of the evening.

But James was too much of a gentleman to ignore Sarah, and he tried hard to look interested as she began plying him with questions. Yet as he did his best to answer them, James felt his spirits plummet, and he stole another, last look at Vanessa.

She was studying him carefully, and their eyes met briefly before Vanessa turned on her heel and exited the parlor, no doubt for the last time that evening.

Blown it! James thought, his shoulders slumped in defeat as he watched Vanessa disappear into the hallway. He'd just lost his one and only chance of the night with her.

And he didn't know when he'd get another. *If ever . . .*

Hello! This is working like a charm! Sarah thought gleefully as she eyeballed her father sitting up and taking notice of her flirt act.

"When you qualify, I am *definitely* going to make you my stockbroker!" Sarah cooed, batting her eyelashes at James and flashing him a coy smile.

They'd been talking about James's investment-banking career, and as she hit James with a slew of eager questions, Sarah had been gratified to spot her father spotting *her* little tête-à-tête! It was all going swimmingly.

Sarah chuckled inwardly. Her father was visibly trying not to eavesdrop, but Sarah could see out of the corner of her eye that he was definitely watching. In fact, she had to force herself not to giggle outright at her dad, who looked rather like a turtle, his neck creeping farther and farther out of his collar with each simpering sentence that came out of Sarah's lips. Perfecto! Sarah congratulated herself. From her own immaculate flirting to her father's pretense at not noticing, it was all very much in keeping with her brilliant plot!

"I still don't get why you're so interested, Sarah," James remarked with a teasing smile. "You couldn't give a rat's bum about investment banking. You're sixteen. Shouldn't you be upstairs, listening to Eminem or whatever scary American's got your fancy now?"

"Jay-ames!" Sarah squealed, and fake punched him on the arm. "Stop telling me what to do!"

Sarah grinned as James pretended to be wounded. Flirting with James wasn't half bad. James was an excellent chap, jolly witty, and easy to talk to, especially for a stuffed shirt from Oxford. He even made banking sound like fun!

"Want some more coffee?" Sarah asked him, snatching at his cup. "I'll get it for you myself," she added.

Yes! Her father had sat bolt upright at that one, and Sarah could detect a broad, ear-to-ear smile on his face even though he was practically across the room, in front of the TV. But the old fish had fallen for the bait. *And he's going to love me for this one,* Sarah thought smugly as she refilled James's cup from the coffeepot on the sideboard. She was the dutiful daughter offering an appropriately upper-class man coffee, as a noblewoman ought. *My father's dream come true!*

With a sly smile Sarah handed James his coffee and perched semiflirtatiously on the arm of a stuffed leather chair. *Don't overdo it!* she cautioned herself. She had to act flirty but not too flirty, just as she had to pretend she wasn't doing this for the earl's benefit.

"Want to split this piece of Black Forest cake?" Sarah asked James, gesturing at the slice of cake she'd brought over from the sideboard. "It's just divine, but I can't eat it all myself!"

Ho ho! Sarah almost clapped as James dug his fork into the cake and her father tried to act like he'd seen nothing. *Speaking of pieces of cake! This whole plan is a piece of cake. A cakewalk . . . as easy as pie!* Sarah felt almost giddy from exhilaration as she drank in the success of her ploy. Things were going so well, she was sure her dad would forgive her by morning and restore all her privileges to her.

Good old Daddy-kins! Sarah thought, carefully keeping her eyes trained on James and away from the earl. *He's playing right into my more than capable hands. . . .*

"You should come back for dinner this weekend," Elizabeth heard Sarah remarking to James. "Lavinia, the blushing bride-to-be, is coming up, so it will all be quite festive."

Lavinia. Elizabeth pricked up her ears at the name, feeling an unexpected twang of nervousness vibrating inside her. Of course, she was also wildly curious. Max's fiancée, the dreaded, supposedly witchlike Lavinia. *I guess we'll meet soon. . . .*

As Elizabeth carefully picked her way around the parlor, collecting empty cups and side plates, she noticed Max almost imperceptibly stiffen as the conversation turned to Lavinia's impending visit. Maybe she was imagining it, but she didn't think so. Max definitely looked a little bit uncomfortable as she met his eyes, and Elizabeth couldn't help wondering whether perhaps she, Elizabeth, had something to do with his discomfort.

Don't kid yourself! Elizabeth scolded herself as soon as the thought crossed her mind. Yet she had to admit it was possible. Max had been watching her ever since she'd entered the room. Elizabeth could feel the current between them. She was pretty sure he felt it too.

But so what! Elizabeth chastised herself for getting carried away, briskly snatching up a stack of empty plates and placing them on a silver tray. *Just because he notices you doesn't mean anything. He's engaged!*

Annoyed with herself, Elizabeth instead concentrated on listening to Sarah, hoping to distract herself from thinking more about Max. *Hard not to be distracted by that voice!* Elizabeth thought, smiling to herself as Sarah shrieked and squealed and generally overflirted with James.

Typical teen! Elizabeth thought. Sarah probably thought she was being subtle, but Elizabeth knew that sixteen wasn't a subtle age. Still, Sarah's cluelessness and slapstick flirting style made her somewhat endearing and less of a brat. In fact, Sarah kind of reminded Elizabeth of how Jessica would have acted not so long ago. . . .

Cut that *thought!* Elizabeth commanded herself,

feeling anger at Jessica burn up inside her as she picked up Sarah's empty cake plate and wiped crumbs from the mahogany coffee table. Thoughts of Jessica were to be avoided at all costs—especially when she had trays of delicate plates to carry!

"Hey, James! This is Elizabeth, from America," Sarah said, suddenly noticing Elizabeth and grabbing at her sleeve. "She's got the craziest name. Elizabeth Bennet, like from *Pride and Prejudice*. Isn't that a scream?"

"I think it's rather chic," Max responded smoothly, and Elizabeth smiled demurely, anxious not to be spotted being overly familiar by the earl. Yet as she looked furtively in Lord Pennington's direction, she was pleased to see him sound asleep and snoring in front of the TV.

"So are your experiences in England anything like you expected?" James asked Elizabeth, genuine interest lighting up his pleasant, intelligent blue-gray eyes.

"Well . . ." Elizabeth looked around, slightly self-conscious to see that Max, James, Sarah, and Victoria were all watching her. "Well, um, no. For starters, no one called Darcy has befriended me," she retorted wittily, creating a ripple of laughter around her. "And the food is much better than I thought it would be!"

Everybody laughed loudly at that one. "Quite

right!" Max said, clapping. "Nothing wrong with bangers and mash!"

"Or toad in the hole!" Sarah piped up.

"Good clotted cream," Elizabeth added, grinning and avoiding looking at Vanessa, who had returned to give the earl his sherry and was coolly regarding Elizabeth from the doorway. But Elizabeth didn't care what Vanessa thought. It was her problem if she didn't want to be civil and join in.

"You're a brick for saying you like our grub," Victoria commented, her plump face dimpling into a smile. "I've been to America, and I *loved* the food. . . ."

This is nice! Elizabeth thought, feeling suddenly more like Elizabeth Wakefield and less like Elizabeth Bennet. These people were talking to her. Really talking to her like she was a part of the group. And it felt good.

"Well, are we *finished* here?" a strident voice broke in, and Elizabeth turned and saw Mary looking disapproving from the door. "Anything else from the kitchen, anyone?"

"No." Sarah spoke up, flicking her eyes away from Elizabeth's. "That'll be all. Elizabeth, you may go," she added brusquely.

A flaming sensation suddenly enveloped Elizabeth's cheeks, and she realized she'd broken out into an awful, embarrassed blush. Not that anyone was looking at her. They'd reverted to their former conversations, leaving her to finish clearing and get out of the room. *What a fool I've been!* Elizabeth thought miserably, humiliation rippling through her as she hurried to pile plates, desperate to get away from the group.

For a moment she'd actually thought these people were interested in her. But they weren't. They were just being polite to the servant girl and didn't have any interest in Elizabeth as a person. Sarah's stinging dismissal had made that absolutely clear. And now Elizabeth was invisible, just a lowly maid, as far as they were concerned.

Max too, Elizabeth thought harshly, berating herself for ever thinking he'd meant anything by his politeness. He was an aristocrat, and she was way beneath him.

Feeling totally put in her place, Elizabeth trembled as she gathered a stack of coffee cups and hastily headed for the door.

"I told you so," Vanessa whispered as she stood aside to let Elizabeth through. Tears welled up in Elizabeth's eyes as she pushed past Vanessa, who trailed her into the kitchen. It was bad enough to be embarrassed in front of everyone. She didn't need Vanessa rubbing her nose in it.

But Vanessa actually looked at her with something faintly resembling sympathy. "Come on,

Elizabeth Bennet," she said in a tone that almost passed for kindness as Elizabeth rinsed the cups and placed the last of the plates in the dishwasher. "Alice wants to give us facials. Pay you back for taking the fall for her mess up yesterday. We shouldn't disappoint her, should we?"

"No," Elizabeth bleated, sniffing back her tears as she and Vanessa made for the servants' staircase. "We shouldn't disappoint Alice."

There'd been enough disappointment for one evening.

Chapter Ten

"Stellar performance from Lady Sarah Pennington!" Sarah mock bowed and pretended to accept a BBC Dramatic Arts award from Victoria, who lay giggling on Sarah's bed.

Sarah bowed again to an imaginary audience of admirers. She ended with a flourish and flipped her long, brown hair back triumphantly. She was feeling very pleased with herself indeed. The flirtation scheme had been nothing short of a roaring success, and it had all been unbelievably easy to execute.

Even James had made it easy. *Quite a worthy costar,* Sarah thought. She'd rather enjoyed flirting with James. He was very charming and quite hot. But even if she could have him—and Sarah knew he was completely stuck on Vanessa and therefore completely unavailable—even if she *could* have him, James wasn't the costar Sarah wanted. That spot had already been taken.

Nicholas Jones . . . Sarah flopped onto her bed beside Victoria and expelled a dreamy sigh tinged with regret as she thought of Nick at the park with his friends right now, probably still hoping against hope that she'd turn up, even though they both knew it wasn't going to happen. *He's the only one I want.*

Nick was everything. Not even Prince William could measure up in terms of general hotness and, well . . . everything. Nick was the total package— minus the title and wealth, of course. *But who cares?* Sarah thought as she picked up the photo of Nick from her nightstand and gazed at it lovingly. She couldn't give a hang about status. *And our family has enough dosh to keep me in Prada for as long as I live!* Sarah thought, half jokingly. Besides, none of that stuff mattered. *Not when it comes to my heart . . .*

"I really cracked it," Sarah gloated to Victoria, remembering the happy look on her father's face as he watched her with James. "What a coup!"

Just then there was a knock at the door. "Come in," Sarah trilled.

"Hello, darling." *Daddy, just as I thought!* Honestly, her father could be so predictable some-times, it was almost boring. "Just wanted to say good night before I turn in," the earl ventured, and Sarah shot him her most syrupy smile.

"Good night, Lord P.," Victoria chirped.

"Sleep tight, Daddy!" Sarah hugged her father tightly and waved him out the door. *Splendid*. She rubbed her hands together. "I predict that in two days, Daddy will let me go out again! He's eating out of the palm of my hand!"

"And let's hope he'll let you have sleepovers again," Victoria added as she slung her school bag over her shoulder and yawned. "I guess we should be glad he let you have me over for dins, but I am *so* not in the mood for going home right now!" she added, checking her watch. Her brother, Lyle, was to pick her up and would be there any minute now.

Suddenly Sarah shot bolt upright on her bed, a mischievous glint in her eyes. "Of course . . . ," she murmured. And, "Yes . . ."

Suddenly everything seemed clear and obvious. She was amazed she hadn't clicked sooner!

"Yes, what?" Victoria prompted. "You look like you just figured out the theory of relativity. Speaking of which, I'd better get some studying in before tomorrow's nasty science exam. . . ."

But Sarah's mind was blitzing through other, more pressing equations. Such as the fact that Lyle was about to pick up Victoria. Such as the fact that their route home passed the Welles School directly. And Nick was in the park right behind the school.

"It's perfect," Sarah explained to Victoria, her eyes shining. "Daddy won't suspect a thing. He just saw me in my pajamas, and he's retired to his suite for the night. All I need to do is grab a lift home, and I'm set!"

"Very sneaky!" Victoria nodded appreciatively, and Sarah felt a rush of energy and excitement at the thought of seeing Nick, of surprising him in the park. The plan was perfect. Lyle was hardly the sharpest tool in the shed, and it would be easy to get him to drop her off at the school. Nothing could go wrong, and the timing couldn't be better!

I'm invincible! Sarah was on a high as she stripped off her pajamas and wiggled into a pair of sexy, hip-hugging Gaultier jeans and a green velvet sweater.

Just then Sarah's intercom buzzed. "It's Lyle," Mary said. "He's just driven up."

Mary . . . Sarah had almost forgotten that potential snag in the plans. "Hang it!" she snapped crossly, looking over at Victoria. "If she busts me, I'm finished!"

"We'll just have to keep her off the scent somehow," Victoria offered, looking serious. But how exactly that would happen, neither of them knew.

And they didn't have time to figure it out. Lyle was downstairs, waiting.

Sarah took a deep breath, snatched a red lipstick from her bureau, slipped it into her pocket, and tied her hair back into a messy I'm-almost-in-bed topknot in case Mary should smell a rat. "You go first," Sarah instructed Victoria. "I'll slip down when it looks safe, and if I have to deal with Mary, I'll cross that big and bulky bridge when I come to it."

"Ten-four. And good luck!" Victoria winked at Sarah and then headed for the stairs.

Sarah stood outside her bedroom door, her heart almost in her mouth. *I'm so close,* she told herself, psyching herself up for her big escape. She *was* so close. Once out of the house and away from Mary, she'd be free. But Sarah felt her mouth go dry as she pictured the consequences of getting caught. The plan was good, but not quite perfect.

And the question was still up in the air: Could she sneak out successfully?

Can I sneak in . . . ? The question went round and round on an endless loop inside Vanessa's head. She couldn't stop thinking about the countess's suite and fretting over whether she'd be able to poke around in it that night after the others were in bed or if it would be too risky. *If I ever get out of here!*

If Vanessa could have rolled her eyes, she would have, but unfortunately she'd let Alice slather her face in some sort of terrifying seaweed and God-knew-what-else combo. *If I move, my face might crack!* Vanessa thought, her hands itching to rip off the mask and get going.

But Alice was determined to finish her facials, had turned their bedroom into a minispa, and was currently too busy smooshing gunk onto Elizabeth to get to Vanessa and help her peel hers off.

At least someone's enjoying this. Through half-opened, seaweed-encrusted lids, Vanessa observed that Elizabeth looked much more relaxed with her face goo on. Not that the girl needed help with her skin, but she'd had a cruddy evening and could clearly use a bit of pampering.

Vanessa bristled under her mask as she thought of that bratty little upstart, Sarah, talking down to Elizabeth as if she were dirt. *Elizabeth, you may go!* Sarah's snippy, hot-potato voice vibrated on the inside of Vanessa's skull. *Little twerp!* Vanessa would have loved nothing more than to slap the girl, and she felt her outrage rising, less from any real caring for Elizabeth and more from a general disgust at having witnessed *yet another* performance from a spoiled Pennington!

"You look awfully hot under the collar, Vanessa," Alice remarked as she patted Elizabeth's cheeks with her concoction. "What's got your knickers in such a knot?"

"Just revisiting fond memories," Vanessa replied caustically. "Another night of aristo*crass!*" Vanessa's eyes burned, sparks flashing as she thought of "Lady" Sarah and her family, who evidently prided themselves on their noble manners when in fact they were as boorish and rude as all get out!

The same undoubtedly went for James. *He's probably negotiating to "buy" me from the Penningtons,* Vanessa imagined, her eyes smarting from either the mask's camphor fumes or her own indignation; she couldn't tell which and didn't much care. Of course, James could never buy her, but Vanessa imagined Max making a joke of that sort and roping James in. And she'd caught James and Max staring at her in the parlor and whispering. As if she wouldn't notice. Who did they take her for, Helen Keller?

It was all so utterly revolting. . . .

"Not all aristocrats are dreadful," Alice attempted to argue. "There were definitely good earls. Useful ones."

"Like who?" Vanessa challenged as Alice directed her to a steaming basin of water in the bathroom and ordered her to put a towel over her head.

"Earl *Grey!*" Alice shot back triumphantly. "The tea earl. He was a good one, a great one, really," she babbled idiotically. "Inventing that tea and all. It's my favorite, it is."

"Oh, for God's sake!" Vanessa retorted, and Elizabeth giggled from the bedroom. "Do you think he made the tea himself, Alice? Picked each leaf with his own two hands? Honestly!"

As the girls chattered on, it was all Vanessa could do not to shake Alice for her naivete. And Elizabeth, for that matter.

"I hope you've finished your initiation into the ways of this house, Elizabeth," Vanessa lectured, after scolding Alice for being so dumb. "You've now seen for yourself how things are, so give up your dreams of nice earls and charming sons. Or else those dreams will crush you!"

Vanessa padded back into the bedroom with a towel as Elizabeth murmured something about having learned her lesson.

"Really, Elizabeth, what were you thinking?" Vanessa snapped as she chewed out Elizabeth for entertaining fantasies about her and Max. "Separate staircases, separate *lives*," Vanessa ranted. "Scullery maid and scion. Pantry and Parliament. Got it?"

Elizabeth nodded. "Trust me, I'm over it," she added vehemently.

"Unless of course you'd like to be Max's tart on the side," Vanessa added coldly. "And then you can join a long line of tradition that has served noblemen throughout history!"

Chastened, Elizabeth shuddered and shook her head again, this time even more vigorously. Vanessa shuddered too, out of disgust for the earl who had used her mother as if she were expendable, as if she were just a bit on the side, good for nothing but a torrid, cheap good time.

"They're a nasty batch!" Vanessa spluttered angrily, tossing the face towel onto her bed. Of course, she couldn't let on to the girls just how nasty the earl really was, but they'd find out soon enough when she blew him out of the water!

"Luckily not even earls are immune to reaping what they sow, however," Vanessa said enigmatically, trailing off into a stony, fierce silence.

"How d'you mean?" Alice demanded. "Reaping what?"

"Let's just say . . ." Vanessa struggled to find the words. "Let's just say that even when life's a bowl of cherries . . . there's always the chance of choking on one," she finished cryptically, strolling over to the window to get a breeze on her hot, steam-scrubbed cheeks.

"Huh?" But Vanessa simply waved Alice off and stared moodily out the window. Even if she wasn't being cryptic, the logically challenged Alice simply wasn't smart enough to follow. Plus Vanessa couldn't elaborate. Her secret had to remain secret . . . for now.

"Well, lookee here." Vanessa craned her neck as she spotted something below. *What's this?*

Sarah, looking all too shifty, had slipped suddenly into the backseat of a waiting car with Victoria.

A slow smile spread across Vanessa's face as she put two and two together. "Seems our *grounded* Lady Sarah is sneaking out," she reported as Elizabeth and Alice leaped over to the window to catch a bird's-eye view of Sarah sliding down in her seat. "Naughty, naughty . . ."

"She's not supposed to be going out," Alice commented, stating the obvious as usual. Sarah's being in disgrace was common knowledge in the house. "Well, this is good fortune," Alice went on, her face lighting up as she turned to the others. "Don't you see? Mary's supposed to be keeping an eye on Sarah. And if I report this to Mary, she'll forgive all the things I've been doing wrong lately. She'll stop getting on me for being so slack, and then I'll be in her good books again!"

"Oh, Alice, don't you think that's mean?" Elizabeth challenged. "Sarah will get into even worse trouble with her father than she already is."

Vanessa studied Elizabeth with grudging admiration. Even after Sarah had cut her down, Elizabeth was still prepared to take the high road.

But though Vanessa internally agreed with Elizabeth and on principle hated tattletales, she was leaning more toward Alice's idea. After all, anything that would snub snotty Sarah in her tracks was a bonus for Vanessa. Plus Alice was toeing a fine line with Mary, and Vanessa felt sorry for the poor twit. She was just so useless that it was hard to imagine her gainfully employed beyond Pennington House.

It's a feel-good choice, Vanessa thought, smirking as she pictured Sarah getting busted by Alice the rat. All very low-level, but it was too tantalizing to resist.

"I think it's cruel," Elizabeth argued with Alice. "I say we don't do it."

Impressive, Vanessa thought, *if a little too nice for my taste . . .* Vanessa watched as the car slowly pulled away and then turned back to Elizabeth and Alice, a chilly smile forming on her lips as the girls looked anxiously at her to see which way the verdict would go. So far it was one all, and Vanessa would be the tiebreaker.

To turn Sarah in or spare her? Vanessa gave it a final glancing consideration before opening her mouth to speak. "Well, my fellow jurors," she began cheerily. "No points for guessing how I'll cast my vote!"

Made it! Sarah exhaled in a huge rush of relief and excitement as she sprinted toward a surprised-looking Nick and hurled herself into his arms.

"I can't believe you're here!" Nick yelped, lifting Sarah easily in his strong arms and finding her mouth with his own.

Like clockwork! As they entered the park, Sarah congratulated herself on yet another scheme gone well. *I'm on a roll!* Sneaking off had been a breeze. Mary was too busy answering phone calls to bother monitoring the door. And then it had been a simple matter of convincing the semicretinous Lyle that she had choir practice . . . and Sarah was home free! *Choir!* Sarah guffawed out loud. She couldn't even sing a note!

"Hi, Sarah!"

Sarah greeted Simon Lake and Fiona Healy, who were draped across each other on a blanket spread across the grass. Simon was a pal of Nick's, a childhood friend who had also grown up in the East End and had left school early to join a rock band.

"Sip?" Fiona disentangled herself from Simon's arms and held out a brown-paper-wrapped bottle of vodka. Two years older than Sarah, Fiona was beautiful in a wild-rebel sort of way and made Sarah shy. She was a scholarship student doing her A levels at Welles, incredibly brainy but also totally cool and edgy with a pierced nose and flaming dyed red hair.

Fiona also had a major rep at school and was rumored to have slept with half the boys at Welles, but Sarah couldn't help admiring her. Everyone did, even Victoria, who normally disapproved of girls like Fiona.

"Come on, sweetie, don't be scared—it's only a nip of vodka!" Fiona giggled, but Sarah shook her head. She knew she was being a goody-goody party pooper, but she had a science exam the next day.

". . . Since I haven't studied, I'd better not make it worse by drinking!" Sarah explained, feeling a pinch of guilt and anxiety about the exam, which she'd almost completely forgotten about. But those feelings were swiftly replaced by a sudden self-loathing. *You sound like a right twit*, Sarah castigated herself. She'd been dying to get a chance to hang out with Nick's cool crowd. But now that she had it, she'd blown it, looking like a nerd and making Nick look like an idiot in the process. Nice going!

"Aw, love, loosen up!" Simon ragged Sarah as Fiona giggled drunkenly. "Maybe a drink would help you out!"

"Lay off!" Nick broke in, pulling Sarah close just as she was considering giving in and grabbing the bottle. "Sarah's got her own mind. She doesn't have to get drunk to prove herself," he added defensively.

"Thass right, she's a lady," Fiona slurred, teasing. "Ah, yes, Lady Sarah Armstrong-Jones or something like that? Lady Sarah Buttermilk-Pancake, is it? I know it's one of those double-barreled names. . . ."

"Ladies can let their hair down, you know," Simon added, holding up the bottle again as he ran a hand through his mod-cut black bowl of hair, slick with pomade. "Unless they don't want to rough around with us plebs."

Crikey! Sarah squirmed with embarrassment. She wasn't able to tell if Simon and Fiona really thought she was a snob or if they were just joking, but either way it made her uncomfortable, like the odd one out. God, it was embarrassing to be an aristocrat around them!

Sarah swallowed, licked her dry lips, and desperately tried to think up a witty, quick response that would make them think she was all right. But nothing would come, even though Sarah could usually count on her sharp tongue to help her along in tricky moments.

But luckily Nick seemed to have less of a problem

verbalizing. "Hey, hold it a sec," Nick shot back, his voice calm but firm. "My girl's a lady not because she was born into it, but because she's a classy person, so cut her a break. And another thing . . ." Nick appeared to be just warming up in his defense of Sarah, and she flushed, touched that he would take this all so seriously. "Sarah's focused and together, and frankly, after all the boozing we've been around growing up in the East End, we could use a change of company, don't you think? Makes for a refreshing change."

Nick's eyes flashed with anger and pride, and Sarah felt like she might melt as he pulled her possessively toward him. *My girl*. He'd called her *my girl*, and the words made her feel woozy.

"Take a chill pill, Jonesy boy," Simon answered with a lazy, pleasant smile. "Fi was just taking the mickey . . . and Sarah, love, if you don't want to drink, suit yourself. All the more for us!"

Nick really does care about me. . . . Sarah barely even heard Simon's words; she was too busy enjoying the feeling of being in Nick's arms, luxuriating in the knowledge that he really, truly thought she was special. Not that she'd ever disbelieved him, but he'd proved it here, now, with everyone watching. He'd stuck up for her in front of his crowd. He was proud of her. *Proud to be* with *me* . . .

Sarah buried her head farther into Nick's leather jacket, inhaling the smell of cigarette smoke, leather, and Nick. *My boyfriend,* she thought proudly, feeling safer, more loved, and more protected than she'd ever felt in her life.

Meanwhile Fiona and Simon had started another drunken conversation and were busy making fun of their other friends' girlfriends.

"Can you believe that Jill McAllister still hasn't done it with Woodsy?" Fiona scoffed, slugging vodka and shaking her head. "She's still a virgin, if you believe." She sniggered. "A virgin!" Fiona smiled exclusively at Sarah and rolled her eyes, sharing the joke.

At that moment Sarah felt deeply thankful that it was nighttime. Because otherwise Fiona would have spotted her telltale scarlet cheeks, blazing with embarrassment.

"If she hasn't done it by now, when is she going to? When she's *married?*" Fiona spluttered into another peal of laughter and then fell drunkenly on Simon, and the two began to make out fiercely, rolling over the grass as they kissed and groped at each other.

Why can't the earth ever open up and swallow you like in storybooks? Sarah wondered miserably, mortified to think of how she'd be roasted if Simon and Fiona found out she was still a virgin.

A nondrinking, nonsmoking aristocratic virgin dating their friend. Sarah thought she'd rather jump off London Bridge than have them know!

"Well, I think people should mind their own damn business," Nick retorted loudly, tightening his arm around Sarah's waist. "Come on then, sweetie. Let's sit on a bench, shall we?"

Still glowing, partly from embarrassment and partly out of gratitude that Nick hadn't spilled the secret of her virginity to any of his friends, Sarah followed Nick to a bench and snuggled into his muscular arms.

The fact that Nick hadn't said anything to anyone about whether he and Sarah were having sex was just further proof that he really loved her. Further proof that she was the luckiest girl in England.

But Sarah was still bothered by the conversation.

Is everyone doing it? she worried. She didn't usually fall for that one, but suddenly Sarah wasn't so sure of herself. Maybe there was more sex going on at school than she knew. And maybe those who weren't doing it were the exception and not the rule!

Alarmed, Sarah raked a shaking hand through her hair, but then she felt a warm, steady palm close over her own, and she felt instantly calmed as Nick stroked her hand and murmured something about not minding his "idiot friends."

"Come here, angel." Nick's voice was hoarse with lust, and as she nestled close to him, Sarah felt his hands slide under her sweater until his fingers gently grazed the skin of her stomach.

Wow! A delicious, tingling sensation shot through Sarah, and she tilted her head, her lips parted. The feel of Nick's warm hands on her stomach was heaven, and Sarah quivered with desire, her mouth meeting Nick's with as much demanding urgency as his own.

Not getting to spend much time with Nick only heightened the excitement Sarah felt in his arms, his lips crushing her own at first, then softening into a slow, lingering, teasing kiss as his hands moved up to caress the muscles in her upper stomach.

"Mmmm . . ." A moan of pleasure escaped Sarah's lips as Nick's hands traced slow circles on her skin. He moved his mouth to her neck, nibbling softly, then gave her neck a light, playful bite. *I'm not sure how much more of this I can stand!* Sarah's breathing was ragged, her mind thick with desire. All she could think of was wanting Nick. Wanting more of him. Wanting all of him.

She didn't care that she was in a park, and suddenly she didn't care about anything that had worried her before. At that moment Sarah just wanted

Nick to make love to her. To own her body just as he owned her heart.

I'm ready, she told herself, moving Nick's hands slowly but decisively up her body, feeling his searching fingers trace the line of her bra. *I'm really ready,* she thought as his hands lingered tantalizingly on her hot skin and his fingers found the clasp on her bra. *I'm . . . not!*

Embarrassed and apologetic, Sarah sat up, closing her hands over Nick's and gently moving his hands away. "I'm sorry," she said in a small voice, her throat suddenly constricting as tears threatened to come. "I'm so . . . so sorry." Sarah's voice broke as she caught a glint of confusion in Nick's eyes and saw him clench the muscles in his jaw. What was wrong with her? She was just confusing him, leading him on. *I'm a tease!* Sarah thought miserably as she averted her eyes from Nick's and put her head in her hands.

What's my problem? Sarah forced away her tears and instead berated herself for ruining a perfectly romantic moment. Her moods were all over the place, and it upset her to know that she was messing with Nick. But Sarah couldn't get a grip. One moment she felt she was on top of the world, and the next she felt unsure, scared, and shaky.

"I'm sorry, Nick, I'm just confused," Sarah admitted, bitterly hoping against hope that he would stay to listen, although if he stalked off right now, Sarah wouldn't blame him. She was one big, confusing road map of mixed signals, and no one could be expected to put up with that for long.

"Hey." Nick's voice was gentle, and his hand cupped her chin, forcing Sarah to look at him. "Don't apologize. You've had a crap week, and if you'd rather talk than kiss, that's what I'm here for!"

"I guess I'm just not sure about anything right now," Sarah murmured, and she grabbed Nick's hand and kissed it forcefully, amazed and gratified that Nick was being so understanding and sensitive to her mood-swing needs. "My whole life feels like a seesaw," Sarah admitted. "One moment things are perfect; the next minute everything's at rock bottom."

"You don't have to be perfect all the time, you know," Nick responded gently. "Sometimes life just goes that way. And just remember you can off-load on me whenever you want. That's what boyfriends are for."

A swell of love expanded like a bubble inside Sarah's chest, and she thought she might burst as she clung to Nick and told him how lonely she felt sometimes. How lately she'd really been missing her mother.

Sarah told Nick how isolated and trapped she

felt at home. How she'd begun to loathe the privilege of her family name. How confused she was about who she was and what she wanted. Before long Sarah and Nick were engaged in a serious conversation about their hopes and dreams and fears.

"I'm not sure what I want to do," Nick said, dragging on a cigarette and staring intensely into the darkness. "But I do know I want to be better than my old man. I want to make something out of my life. Sometimes I think about studying architecture. I fantasize about building amazing public spaces in crappy neighborhoods like where I grew up so that everyone can have something beautiful to look at. Probably sounds stupid, but there it is. My dream . . ." Nick trailed off, looking slightly embarrassed, and Sarah's heart lurched.

"I think that sounds amazing," she whispered, clasping Nick's hand tightly. It did sound amazing to Sarah. It was also amazing to her to think that they could talk so easily about anything and everything. Being attracted to each other was one thing, but Sarah had always dreamed of having a boyfriend who was also her best friend. Someone exactly like Nick.

"So how about you? What do you want to be?" Nick asked Sarah, and she shrugged.

"Haven't the faintest. But I know what I *don't*

want to be. Someone like Lavinia. She's just a typical aristocrat, her whole boring life neatly mapped out. A life of going to galas and balls where she gets to talk to other people exactly like her. Ugh!" Sarah wrinkled her nose in disgust and shook her head at the image of herself living like Lavinia. "I want my life to be exciting and unpredictable. I want to take chances, not sit back and let everything happen to me."

"I hear you," Nick replied, nodding seriously. Then he wrapped his arms around Sarah's waist and pulled her into his lap. "But somehow I doubt your life will be boring, Lady Sarah Pennington." Nick touched the tip of Sarah's nose. "You've got too much fire in you, angel. No one can put it out."

How did I find him? Sarah gazed back at Nick, amazed that during all the confusing months she'd gone through ever since she turned sixteen, she'd still somehow managed to connect to this incredible person who made her feel like she could do anything and be anything. And he would be right there next to her, supporting her and loving her.

"I don't deserve you," Sarah murmured as Nick cradled her head on his shoulder. "But now that I have you, I'm keeping you," she added with a happy sigh.

Right there, with her head on Nick's shoulder,

everything felt like it made sense. They just felt right together, and at that moment Sarah wondered why she'd felt hesitant about taking the next step with Nick.

She looked up at him, and then they were kissing again, a long, passionate kiss that made Sarah feel like a million tiny fireflies were dancing up and down her spine.

"Back to the subject of taking chances . . . ," Nick began as they broke away, their eyes still locked. "Have you made a decision yet? Will you let me make love to you, Sarah?" Nick's voice was husky and serious, and he gripped Sarah's hands in his own. "I know you're scared, but I promise you, you won't regret it if you say yes."

"I . . . have made my decision." Sarah took a deep breath, feeling suddenly like time had stopped still and all there was were Nick's eyes looking into hers, his hands locked together with hers so tightly that she didn't know whose fingers were whose. *No one in the world but us . . .*

And my bloody cell phone!

"Hold on," Sarah muttered apologetically as she scrambled through her pocket, looking for the source of the annoying ring. "It's just Vic," she added. "She said she'd call to make sure I was okay. I'll be quick."

Sarah snapped open the cell phone without

breaking the intense, loving gaze between her and Nick. *Trust Vic to pick the wrong moment!* Sarah thought with a rueful smile, preparing to cut Victoria's chatter as quickly as she could so as to get back to the romantic private moment Sarah was so eager to share.

"All clear!" Sarah said triumphantly into the phone.

"I'm afraid not," the voice on the other end replied acidly, and Sarah felt her blood run cold and her stomach twist into a sickeningly tight ball of fear and shock. Because it wasn't Victoria on the line.

It was Lord Pennington.

Chapter
Eleven

"He's going to murder me!" Sarah gulped tearfully, clinging to Nick's arm as she stumbled toward the park gate. Her whole body felt like one big tremor, and she was still recovering from the shock of her father's icy fury on the telephone. He hadn't even let her speak, had simply demanded to know where she was and ordered her to stay put until he got there. Then he'd hung up without another word. And somehow that silence felt worse to Sarah than if her father had yelled.

But the awful angry silence was nothing compared to what Sarah knew awaited her any minute now, when she and her father would come face-to-face. The earl was on his way, and as she pictured him in his dressing gown, careening across the roads, his face crimson with rage, Sarah was terrified out of her wits.

"You can't leave me," Sarah pleaded with Nick as they reached the park gate. "Not yet. I need you here."

"I'll only split when he gets here. Don't cry. It'll all blow over," Nick soothed, but Sarah couldn't hold back her tears, and a fresh round of sobs racked her body.

"You don't know my father." She sniffled into Nick's jacket. "You can only push him so far, and when you cross the line, he completely loses it!"

And I've really crossed the line now! Sarah thought miserably. Clashing with her father once or twice was bad, but this last transgression would be the straw that broke the camel's back. If there was one thing her father hated, it was deviousness, and Sarah pictured his mounting anger as he drove the highways, picturing her sweetly bidding him good night in her pajamas only to change clothes the minute his back was turned and slip out of the house and into the night. . . .

"I'm really done for," Sarah wept, clutching Nick tightly to her. "And so are we."

If her father made good on his threat to home school her, she'd never get to see Nick again. Her life would be nonexistent, and their relationship would be over.

"Listen here, Sarah." Nick pulled away and regarded her intently. "I won't accept that. Your father can punish you as much as he likes, but he can't get between us, no matter what he does."

"Why do I find that hard to believe?" Sarah responded gloomily. She wished she could believe in Nick's words, but she knew her father would never let her out of the house now. Not after this.

"Look at it this way," Nick continued calmly as Sarah hiccuped back a fresh flood of tears. "He can try to control *you*. But he can't control *me*. And I swear it, if I have to climb through your window myself, I will see you this weekend. We have a date, right?"

As he looked at her, Sarah could see the loving conviction in Nick's eyes. "We're together, Sarah, and that's what counts," he murmured as car headlights rounded the corner and beamed into view. "Nothing and no one can keep us apart."

Sarah swallowed anxiously as the oncoming car lights brightened, looming ever closer while Nick's eyes searched hers eagerly for an answer. Would they be together that weekend? That was what he was asking, and Sarah knew she had to give him her answer now because she might not get another chance.

"This weekend?" Nick prompted. "Are we on?"

The lights of the Rolls-Royce came closer and closer, and Sarah began to panic, picturing her father's imminent rage, especially if he saw Nick standing there.

But Sarah still felt a twinge of fear at the thought of making love to Nick. There could be no going back from there.

Nick's face was inches from her own, the car had begun to slow to a stop, and Sarah's pulse raced with the pressure of the moment. She wanted to give herself to Nick completely, but she also wanted to be sure.

But at that moment Sarah realized that nothing in life was sure. Life was a series of moments, of opportunities you could either seize or turn down.

"Will you?" Nick repeated, his eyes boring into Sarah's with a burning intensity.

"Yes," Sarah breathed, at the very moment that the car came to a dead stop. "Yes, I will. And Nick?"

"Yes?" He squeezed her shoulders.

"Run!"

"She has really done it this time!" the earl boomed, pacing angrily up and down the length of his study. "This is it—I tell you I've had it with your sister, Max!"

Max nodded, knowing there was nothing much he could say to cool his father off. But at the very least he'd managed to convince his father not to fetch her himself. "You're too angry to drive," Max had said when his father had come to him with Mary's report that Sarah had slunk out of the house.

It was true that his father was too angry to drive, and Max had been relieved when the earl relented and dispatched Fenwick to do the honors instead. *This buys us a little time,* Max mused, trying to figure out how best to calm his father before Sarah got back.

But the earl was right. Sarah really had done it this time, and Max shook his head, annoyed that his sister would be that stupid. She deserved punishment, and Max knew she would get it. But he also wanted to protect Sarah. Home schooling wasn't the way to go, and he had only minutes to convince his father of it.

"She'll just get worse, Dad," Max tried to explain as his father ranted about home schooling, pacing up and down the study and jerking his head every so often to look for the car. "I know you're livid, but you have to be careful not to go overboard."

"In the park at all hours of the night!" the earl roared. "It's *midnight,* Max! She could have been *killed* by some maniac!"

"But she's fine, Dad," Max soothed, trying to coax his father into a lower temperature than his current boiling point. "She's just a teenager. They all do that."

"Well, I won't have it!" The earl shook his fist in the air. "It's that Nicholas boy! He's clearly responsible for this. The chump probably has a *nose ring!*"

Max sighed, worrying that Sarah had truly dug her own grave this time by being so willful. In that way she was exactly like their father—stubborn and hotheaded. Which was why Max needed to be there. To defuse the situation somehow. If indeed it was even possible.

"That girl is going to give me a heart attack!" the earl ranted, and Max shook his head, trying to think up something calming to say. His father was seething with rage, but Max knew his rage was mostly a mask for his concern. The earl adored Sarah and felt so much guilt that she had no mother. And in a way that guilt had made him overprotective of her.

Poor Dad. Max could tell that his father was under serious stress. It wasn't easy for him to deal with a teenage daughter, and he didn't have the first clue how to connect to her. Which only made Sarah act out even more. *It's all a vicious cycle,* Max thought disconsolately as he poured his father a shot of whiskey, hoping that would have a calming effect.

214

But as the earl picked up his whiskey glass, the lights of the Rolls-Royce lit up the windowpane. And he put the glass down, too angry and full of anticipation to drink.

"How *dare* she!" he shouted as the car door slammed and footsteps clattered through the house. "Your sister is a disgrace to herself and to this family!"

Here goes . . . Max tugged his hair as he desperately tried to think up some strategy to ease the confrontation that was about to take place, but he knew his father was too upset to listen to reason.

And by the time a whimpering Sarah entered the earl's study, Max knew his father was about ready to throttle her.

"Don't even try it," the earl roared as Sarah attempted to speak. "You're a liar, so why should I listen to anything you have to say?"

"Dad—," Max interjected, holding out his hands. "Keep your voice down. You'll wake the staff."

But the earl was too angry to listen and only increased the volume of his yelling. "You are compromising your moral character with every step!" The earl wagged his finger inches from Sarah's chastened face. "I know where you're headed, young lady!"

At that Sarah suddenly snapped out of appearing apologetic and stared her father in the eye, her eyes flashing. "How do you know where I'm headed?" she spat. "You don't know anything about me. You don't know what's in my heart, and even if you did, you wouldn't care!"

Sarah blinked, tears running down her cheeks, and Max felt his heart go out to her. She *was* behaving terribly, but she was also just a confused teenage girl trying to figure herself out, and obviously their father's anger had struck a nerve.

But the earl wasn't about to go easy on Sarah and glared at her, stone-faced, unmoved by her tears. "It doesn't matter what you think," he began in a low, calm, yet icy voice. "Because the thinking and decision making are now in my hands. If your poor mother could see this . . ." The earl blanched, looking suddenly shaky, then recovered and resumed his stern look.

"If my mother could see this, she'd defend me!" Sarah wailed, but the earl remained impassive and began pacing again, up and down the length of the study.

"You've proved yourself to be incapable of carrying yourself like the young lady that you are," the earl continued, his eyes cold and distant. "Therefore you will remain in your room without any social interaction whatsoever. Since you're behaving like a child, you'll be treated like a child."

Oh, cripes . . . Max stiffened. Clearly his father

was going through with his home-schooling threat, which would unquestionably be an unbelievably disastrous move. Max could just picture the pressure in the house with Sarah in it 24/7. Both Sarah and her father would spontaneously combust! They'd never make it!

"You will be taken to school and picked up directly after," the earl continued, and Max breathed a sigh of relief as he noted that his father had listened to him and done the sensible thing. "You will not be allowed to keep a cell phone. In short, your privacy is completely over."

"You can't do that!" Sarah burst out, and Max shot her a warning look, but she ignored it. *Be glad it's not worse!* he messaged silently to her, amazed that she was acting so stubbornly even though her father had mercifully spared her from home schooling. But Sarah still looked like she'd been run over by a steamroller. *Probably the cell-phone thing,* Max thought with amusement. What was it with girls and phones? If their ears weren't glued to them, they felt like life wasn't worth living!

"Watch me!" the earl answered Sarah, adding that if she even so much as picked up a telephone, a tutor would be on the doorstep to home school her the very next day.

"I hate you!" Sarah sobbed, and Max looked with alarm from Sarah to the earl, searching for something to say to de-escalate the enormous tension in the room, but Sarah broke it first by turning on her heel and flouncing out of the study, sobbing loudly and uncontrollably, her father shouting after her in vain.

"I'm at the end of my tether," the earl confessed to Max after Sarah had left. "I will not allow any child of mine to run wild like this," he added as he lifted his whiskey glass with a shaking hand and took a sip.

"I hear you, Dad," Max replied sympathetically, feeling sorry for his father. The earl looked rather the worse for wear and at almost sixty years of age probably wasn't in the best position to be dealing with a sixteen-year-old daughter.

"One more incident and it's home schooling," he added, his voice harsh with the threat. "Although that would probably only make matters worse," he admitted, shaking his head with the futility of it all.

"Things are bad enough now," Max agreed, imagining Sarah undoubtedly heaving with sobs on her bed, vowing to get back at her father.

Silly, impulsive Sarah! Max mused, pouring himself a whiskey shot. Sarah really was out of her mind sometimes. But then, what teenage girl wasn't?

Max frowned as he stared at the contents of his whiskey glass, wondering how it would all play out from here. Sarah only seemed to get worse when her father clamped down on her, and that didn't bode well, considering the earl's latest, harshest crackdown. *Sarah's already made some big mistakes . . . ,* Max reflected.

He could only hope she wouldn't be driven to make more.

Sweet dreams! Vanessa grinned as she paused outside Mary's door and heard the rumble of her snores. *Finally!* It had taken forever to hear that sound. After Alice went to Mary with the news of Sarah's escape, there was commotion throughout the house, and Vanessa had begun to seriously doubt the possibility of sneaking around undetected.

Yet at last Mary was safely stashed between the sheets, and Vanessa could slip away without worrying about running into Mary in the passage.

Quick as lightning, Vanessa darted silently down the stairs two flights to the second floor, her flashlight in hand. She paused on the landing, just a few feet away from the countess's suite, and fingered the key in the pocket of her robe.

Vanessa stared at the mahogany door in front of her, her fingers itching to fling it open. *If I have to stay in there all night, I will!* Vanessa vowed, lifting her chin, a surge of adrenaline kicking through her.

She felt tremendously focused, much more so than on her previous nights of detective work. *Maybe it's Alice's refreshing facial,* Vanessa thought with a smile, doubting that notion as soon as it came to her. But whatever the reason, she felt charged and eager to make a completely thorough search of the countess's suite. Absolutely everything would be microscopically examined for proof of the affair. Proof had to be there.

And if it isn't there, then the night still won't be in vain, Vanessa reasoned. It would simply narrow down the search. Because Vanessa could feel it in her gut—there was *something* material in that house that would corroborate her story. She just had to find it.

But not before she did a quick check to make sure that the earl was in his suite and preferably asleep. With the countess's suite being on the same floor as Lord Pennington's, Vanessa knew she couldn't be too careful, and she padded quietly in the direction of the earl's wing, keeping her ears open for suspicious noises.

Damn! As she neared the earl's suite, Vanessa was annoyed to hear voices—distant voices at first, but as she walked down the corridor, they grew louder. One of them was clearly the earl's, and if he was in his bedroom, having a telephone conversation or chatting to Max, Vanessa knew she'd have to abort her plans. It was simply too risky to attempt to slip into the countess's suite while others were awake on the very same floor.

Back to square one! Vanessa thought angrily, fuming at the thought of having to halt her quest on account of the earl.

But as she approached the earl's door, Vanessa realized the muffled sounds were coming from the floor below, directly below the earl's rooms. *His study!* she deduced, her spirits lifting as she heard sounds of urgent chatter. The earl's voice, then another deep voice—obviously Max's. Vanessa couldn't make out what they were saying, but the conversation sounded heated. Especially when a third, higher voice chimed in—Sarah's. That voice was immediately cut off by a loud, booming roar. Unmistakably the earl again!

All is not well with the royals! Vanessa chuckled softly as she figured out what all the fuss was about. Not only were the fireworks below pleasing to her personally—any dissent between the Penningtons gave her a little kick—but the goings-on also meant she'd be free to do her sleuthing without fear of being caught. Clearly the family was engaged in a major row—one didn't have to hear the words to catch on to that—and with everyone on the floor below, Vanessa was free to do her work.

Plus there was the added bonus of all the shouting voices. The family discussion had now reached a high-decibel volume, and if it stayed that way, it would act as a kind of detection device for Vanessa, reassuring her of the family's whereabouts.

But just as Vanessa turned to retrace her steps and begin her assignment, she heard the earl shouting Sarah's name, followed by the loud bang of a door.

Then Vanessa heard footsteps, presumably Sarah's, and what sounded like sobbing.

Vanessa smiled at the thought of Sarah sniffling back to her room. *Serves you right!* The brat deserved a bad ending to her evening after acting like Lady Muck all day, but though Vanessa was enjoying the moment on one level, a tiny ripple of a frown furrowed her brow as she realized the family row might be drawing to a close.

Listening closely, Vanessa tried to hear traces of murmuring conversation from the study, but the sound was even more muffled than before, perhaps because the door had been slammed shut.

Not good . . . as Vanessa weighed the possible scenarios going on downstairs, she began to realize that the situation might jeopardize her own plans for the evening. For all she knew, the argument was over—the slamming door could have signaled the end of it. Which would mean that any moment now the earl might come up the stairs. And who knew how long it would take before he cooled off and got to sleep?

Or maybe he'll go after Sarah, Vanessa mused. But that didn't do Vanessa much good either. With all the possible carryings-on in the house, it would take ages for everyone to settle down in their own rooms. The earl's blood was up, Sarah was having a teen attack, and with everyone stomping around, Vanessa knew she was at risk of being caught.

And what possible explanation could she give if she *was* caught wandering around with a flashlight?

Scowling, Vanessa weighed her options, such as they were. She could go ahead with her search and possibly get nabbed by a Pennington or postpone it.

Until when?

Vanessa had delayed enough, and time was precious. She had to get ahead with her search. Everything depended on it.

But though frustrated, Vanessa also knew she had to exercise caution. If she got caught, the game was over.

Of course, every secret search carried an element of risk with it. Shouldn't she just go ahead and worry about trouble when it stared her in the face?

Make a decision! Vanessa knew that each second spent thinking was a second she could have spent in the countess's suite.

But on the other hand, a wrong move on this night and Vanessa knew she would forfeit her chance to find the truth. Forfeit six months of working in the house. Forfeit her one chance to know who she really was.

And then she'd never know.

Chapter
Twelve

Why even pretend to sleep? Sarah thought miserably as she lay stiff as a board between her bedsheets.

She glanced over at the bedside clock: 4 A.M. Not a sound in the house. It was as still as the grave. And as far as Sarah was concerned, every bit as suffocating.

She sat up, ran a hand across her salt-streaked cheeks, and got out of bed. Her head pounded like a sledgehammer, thoughts rushing this way and that, everything a long, muddled string of question marks. Her heart was another matter. It was all one emotion. One very decisive emotion: anger.

You can't keep me in here! Sarah bristled, silently addressing her father, who was no doubt sleeping like a log instead of tossing and turning guiltily like he ought to be. Like he would be if he were a normal father in a normal house instead of a tyrant in a castle.

Sarah grabbed a sweater, slipped it on over her nightgown, picked up her CD Walkman, and climbed out the window. Of course there was no way she could leave the cursed house, but she could at the very least perch on the roof. Which was her favorite place. A tiny square of slate just outside her window, where she'd always gone when she felt sad. Or needed to think. Or both, like now.

As Sarah flipped on the Walkman, the sounds of 'N Sync blasted her away from the stillness and into another space, where love was all that mattered and nothing else existed.

In the distance, over the thick ridge of forest that loomed, sealing the estate from the road, a pale, anemic moon hovered, a sliver of moonlight picking up a spooky fog that hovered over the grounds. At night, like this, the place was creepier than by day, and Sarah felt like she could be back in another era, living on Wuthering Heights. Waiting for her Heathcliff.

Hopefully with a happier ending, she thought gloomily as she recalled Cathy and Heathcliff's doomed love affair in that famous Brontë story of forbidden love.

Right now Sarah could totally identify with Cathy and felt like if she couldn't have Nick, she might also just as well lie down and die.

Wiping away a tear, Sarah tried to figure out how everything had suddenly gone so wrong. She'd never had a row quite this bad with her father. Of course, he'd always been from another century, but then, most girls' fathers were, and even if the earl had got on her case many times before, Sarah had always felt loved by him.

But now it felt like they lived on different planets. Or like she was stuck behind bars and Lord Pennington was her jailer. The enemy.

Sarah still couldn't believe some of the awful things her father had said to her, and she shivered in the darkness beneath her thin sweater, reliving Lord Pennington's brutal words.

I know where you're headed, young lady! Sarah recoiled as she pictured her father's face contorted in anger, his finger wagging in her face. *What was* that *supposed to mean?*

Actually, she knew exactly what her father was getting at. He didn't need to say the words—Sarah could see on his face that he already thought of her as some teen harlot. *A slattern. That's probably the word he had in mind!*

No doubt the earl thought Sarah was sleeping her way around the school, boozing it up in the park, and otherwise acting like someone who didn't even respect herself.

Compromising your moral character . . . her father's words echoed through her skull, and Sarah felt a fresh rush of anger and frustration cresting inside her. *Thanks, Dad,* she thought bitterly, gazing unhappily into the fog. *Thanks for having such a high opinion of me.*

It wasn't that Sarah thought she'd done nothing wrong. But the earl's disappointment and anger were way, way out of proportion to what she had in fact done. It was almost as if he *wanted* to believe the worst of her. Or that he couldn't imagine her actually behaving like an adult.

Which all led Sarah to this depressing, hurtful conclusion: Her father didn't believe in her.

Sarah felt her throat swell and close, another wave of tears rising thick and heavy from deep inside. She'd felt alone lately—had had her weak moments—but she'd never felt this alone, and as tears made their tracks down her cheek, a familiar, desperate longing for her mother came over Sarah. A yearning for the woman she remembered, who had always thought the best of her and had always stuck by her. Had been there when she needed her.

Except that now she was gone, and she was never coming back.

Her mother would have understood. She would have given Nick a chance too instead of deciding against him without even meeting him.

But instead Sarah had to face up to the fact that she was without support. Her father had let her know, in no uncertain terms, just how little he thought of her. He thought she was a write-off. She could see it in his eyes.

I just need to learn not *to care what he thinks!* Sarah decided, purposefully brushing away her tears. If the earl thought she was low, she would have to rise above him. Be independent emotionally. Learn to ignore the cold clutch of her heart when faced with her father's disappointment.

Maybe that's what growing up is all about, Sarah reflected bitterly. Maybe it was about accepting things you couldn't change in those who were supposed to love you. Accepting the fact that they might not think you were worthy of respect even if you knew that in your heart you weren't a bad person and hadn't done anything so sinfully wrong.

Yes, Sarah concluded. She had to stop caring what her dad thought. Cut him out, write him off, as he had done to her.

What does he even know about my life anyway? Sarah wondered, furious that her father could think she was a good-for-nothing when he didn't even know the first thing about her. *And it's still* my *life!*

Sarah had stopped crying by now and regarded the still, ghostly view in front of her with a stoic stare, hugging her knees to her chest as she puffed out the cold air. The eaves had grown damp underneath her, but she felt like she was made of wood and didn't plan on budging anytime soon. Not until she'd frozen her father out of her head completely. Not until she knew for sure that once she reentered that bedroom, she would be her own person, freed from being hurt by her father's callous treatment of her and low estimation of what she was worth.

Sarah considered her father's words again, willing herself not to cry as she pictured him raging at her, telling her how he would take all her decisions away from her and make them himself.

But there were some he couldn't make. Like the one Sarah herself had made that very night with Nick.

You're behaving like a child . . . , the earl had shouted at Sarah. *Well, then, maybe it's time to become a woman,* Sarah answered silently, her eyes tearless and distant.

And the more she thought about it, the more Sarah knew she'd chosen the right path for herself. She would make love to Nick. She would squash all her misgivings and just do it.

It would be a moment of love. Her own private moment, her own special milestone that she could forever treasure in her heart. And no matter how her father treated her from here on out, Sarah could always cling to the fact that Nick loved her, and nothing could change that. *Sticks and stones . . .* , she thought as an image of her father's flushed face appeared before her for the final time. The wagging finger, the angry eyes. *Sticks and stones.*

Even just thinking those words made Sarah feel stronger. Bolder. More independent. It was like a mantra, and the more she said it to herself, the better she felt.

She didn't need her father's love anymore, and she could no longer afford to consider him. She had her own life to live.

And it would start this weekend when she made love to Nick for the first time.

Sarah felt a piercing, shooting pain slicing through her heart. Or maybe it was pleasure. She couldn't tell, but as she pictured Nick lying next to her, his taut body and golden skin naked against her own skin, Sarah felt like she had a window on her own destiny. A vision of the future.

A vision of that very weekend.

She didn't know how exactly she would make their weekend tryst happen, but Sarah knew that somehow, some way, she would.

And there wasn't a damned thing her father could do to stop her . . .

You'll always remember your first love.

Love Stories

Looking for signs he's ready to fall in love?

Want the guy's point of view?

Then you should check out *Love Stories*. Romantic stories that tell it like it is—why he doesn't call, how to ask him out, when to say good-bye.

Love Stories

Available wherever books are sold.

Check out the **all-new**....

Sweet Valley Web site—

www.sweetvalley.com

New Features

Cool Prizes

The ONLY official Web site!

Hot Links

And much more!